PENGUIN BOOKS

THE SWEETS OF PIMLICO

A. N. Wilson was born in Staffordshire and grew up in Wales. *The Sweets of Pimlico* was his first novel and was awarded the John Llewelyn Rhys Memorial Prize for 1978. His other novels are *Unguarded Hours*, *Kindly Light*, *The Healing Art* (Penguin, 1982), which won the Somerset Maugham Prize for 1980, the Southern Arts Literature Prize for 1980 and the Arts Council National Book Award for 1981, *Who Was Oswald Fish?* (Penguin, 1983), *Wise Virgin* (Penguin, 1984), which received the W. H. Smith Annual Literary Award for 1983, and *Gentlemen in England* (Penguin, 1986). He has also written a study of Sir Walter Scott, *The Laird of Abbotsford*, which won the John Llewelyn Rhys Memorial Prize for 1981, biographies of John Milton and Hilaire Belloc (Penguin, 1986) and the non-fiction work *How Can We Know?* (Penguin 1986). His most recent novel, published in Penguin, is *Love Unknown*. He has edited Sir Walter Scott's *Ivanhoe* for the Penguin Classics. A. N. Wilson is a Fellow of the Royal Society of Literature.

A.N. WILSON

THE
SWEETS
OF
PIMLICO

PENGUIN BOOKS

PENGUIN BOOKS

Published by the Penguin Group
27 Wrights Lane, London w8 5TZ, England
Viking Penguin Inc., 40 West 23rd Street, New York, New York 10010, USA
Penguin Books Australia Ltd, Ringwood, Victoria, Australia
Penguin Books Canada Ltd, 2801 John Street, Markham, Ontario, Canada L3R 1B4
Penguin Books (NZ) Ltd, 182–190 Wairau Road, Auckland 10, New Zealand

Penguin Books Ltd, Registered Offices: Harmondsworth, Middlesex, England

First published by Martin Secker & Warburg Ltd 1977
Published in Penguin Books 1983
Reprinted 1985, 1988

Printed and bound in Great Britain by
Cox & Wyman Ltd, Reading
Set in Bembo

For
John Bayley and Iris Murdoch

I

"That affected shit."

Evelyn knew what her brother meant about Geoffrey. That had been months ago. It was humiliating to admit to herself that she had had an affair with such a person: one of those toffee-nosed young men, educated at boarding-schools no one has heard of, and full of themselves as a result. And those teeth.

"Why not tell him to piss off?" Again, fraternal advice, given months back. She now wished that she had. Even more shaming than the affair itself, was that Geoffrey got in first to end it. And, of course, it had to be on the telephone, just when her ears were full of shampoo.

"In Hampshire?"

"*Enamoured*. If you can't be serious, there is perhaps no point in talking."

"The line's awfully bad. Speak up, why can't you."

"I'm going back to her, Evelyn. It's no use pretending. One can't stop these things happening. One must accept it."

"Hullo? Where did you say you were going?"

"I'm going back to Cambridge. We're probably going to get married, Tiff and I."

"To Cambridge? You said a moment ago she lived in America."

"Cambridge, Mass."

"*Speak up*. Cambridge has what?"

"I know you're upset, but why can't we be sensible? Massachusetts. I'm going back to Massachusetts."

"That's what I thought you said. But what was that about Cambridge?"

"There's no point in our seeing one another before I go. I'm leaving on Wednesday."

"It seems rather dismal to part on the telephone."

"We've rather come to an end. It's better not to linger out the agony."

"Couldn't we meet just once before you go?"

"It's better not to."

"Hullo?"

"I said it's better not to."

"Just as you like. It seems a bit sad. After three years, or whatever it is."

"Quick endings are less painful. Their very crispness has a sort of beauty about it."

"*Merry Christmas?* It's only April. Geoffrey, old thing, are you all right?"

"I never liked your calling me 'old thing'. The past three years have meant a lot to me . . ."

"Geoffrey. Geoffrey, are you still there?"

"I love you."

"Geoffrey? We can't part like this. You've still got my copy of Darwin's *Voyage of the Beagle*. Geoffrey? Oh, damn you."

The line had gone dead. That had been a week ago, and she had more or less recovered now. But the whole rigmarole of her three years with Geoffrey had been habit-forming, and since the telephone call, she was fragile. There were large gaps in her days, which she felt obliged to fill, for fear of another ridiculous adventure taking the place of what they called her "love" affair. She decided to take an emotional holiday, to concentrate on the cerebral and the external.

2

The worst thing was that everyone thought she had been "dropped". People had been "kind" to her, avoiding the mention of Geoffrey's name, or alluding to him in tactful, hushed tones.

It *was* odd, his going to America so suddenly. And it appeared to be true, if his account was to be relied on, that he had "fallen in love" there a year or so before, while he was attending a course on American law at Princeton. People looked touched when she imparted this information. Actually, it meant very little to Evelyn. She did not know who this Tiff was, who was supposed to have captured Geoffrey's heart; and the whole phraseology of the situation puzzled her. For all she knew, it might be a black girl. Many Americans were. "Falling in love" was a phrase which had to be used, but which had little exchange value in her vocabulary. She knew that one could be successful or unsuccessful in affairs of the heart, and that being "dropped" was like failing examinations or being bad at tennis: the sort of thing of which her father disapproved.

"What's happened to that barrister friend of yours?" he had asked suspiciously some weeks before, on the last occasion she had been home.

"Couldn't you *see* that Geoffrey and she aren't in love any more?" she had heard her mother saying crossly to Sir Derek when they both thought she was out of earshot.

It was characteristic of her mother to introduce a new element into the conversation, and to combine emotional "interpretation" of her family's characters with rebuking her husband. Before she heard the comment, it had not occurred to Evelyn that her parents had devoted any thought to "her and Geoffrey". Now that the affair was over, she assumed that the family had suffered a little blow to its dignity: a setback, which would take a certain amount of "living down". It was not as if Geoffrey was the first young man who had not "come to anything".

But the disgrace was only a part of the trouble. She felt bored, and at a loose end.

Since she came down from Newnham a couple of years before,

Geoffrey had been her constant companion. She had other friends, of course. She had her job, teaching mathematics in a private school for girls in Knightsbridge. But Geoffrey had taken up most of her time.

He had been a year ahead of her at Cambridge, and by the time she arrived in London, he was already beginning to make a career for himself as a Chancery lawyer. She did not know how this was achieved, but she assumed having an uncle who was a judge had something to do with it. He had always said, before all this Tiff nonsense cropped up, that no one was well educated enough to appreciate Chancery Law unless they had passed through Lincoln's Inn. He was given to such generalisations.

And now, absurdly, how one missed them. It was hard to say in great detail how she had spent her time with Geoffrey. But, at their best moments, they had enjoyed themselves. London had seemed fun. Although they went to concerts occasionally, and mooned around galleries a good deal in wet weather, their lives were not, in lines he liked to quote, "crowded with culture". That had never been Evelyn's style. She was entirely unaesthetic, but she liked to have things explained.

They spent much of their time, when not trying to repair their sex life, just walking in streets and parks, making of London a shared joke, of which she did not always get the point, a shared fantasy world of their own. From week to week, Geoffrey's enthusiasms changed. At one time, it was Butterfield churches; at another, shops whose merchandise still appeared in the window labelled with the old currency. Although the jokes were sometimes difficult for her to perceive, the accumulation of fact which these expeditions involved was consoling to her. Fact was the only thing capable of arousing anything like a passion in her at the moment.

She was at a loose end because it was April, and the school holidays. Her pupils, and problems such as the Binomial Theorem, would have provided a wholesome distraction from the sheer embarrassment which still sickened her. For it was embarrassing,

4

merely embarrassing, to have discovered that Geoffrey had been just a habit. She should have dropped him years before. She knew that most of the world shared her mother's vision of life as a process interrupted by sensations normally designated "love". But she noticed that she was unable to pine for Geoffrey. His absence was irritating; the way he had chosen to leave, more so. But it was more the lack of a companion than the lack of *him* which annoyed her. She felt herself deficient in some natural human function, not to be able to pine more. It seemed possible that she had a heart of stone, and the thought faintly appalled her. People with hearts of stone could not be, ordinarily speaking, nice; and she longed to be nice.

Fact was her only refuge. Each morning, since it was a harsh April, she stayed indoors and read books from the Public Library about Natural History. In the afternoons, however fierce the weather, she walked in Kensington Gardens and repeated to herself the names of at least half a dozen of the species that she had been studying in the morning. If she walked without such a fixed train of thought, her brain wandered; angry thoughts about Geoffrey, or daydreams about her own character, fruitless musings both, passed into the mind.

Natural History was, too, more *use* than a lot of the fancy Geoffrey indulged in. He had always mocked her for her interest in insects. But insects were a jolly sight more comprehensible than, say, architecture. "It is exquisitely bad," Geoffrey had once said to her, writhing with mirth on her arm as they stood by the font in the church of St Augustine's, Queensgate. She had felt mildly disconcerted.

At present, she was trying to memorise the names, Latin and English, of six water-beetles every afternoon.

It was while she was so engaged, near the Round Pond, that she met Mr Gormann.

The wind blew in icy gusts, so strong and cold that one caught one's breath and felt unable to move without pain; like the weather on lacrosse afternoons. And then the wind would suddenly subside, leaving one gasping.

Hydrous piceous, the Great Silver Beetle. The sexes of this species are distinguished by the end joints of the feet or *tarsi* of the front leg, which are triangular on the male, and on the female . . . For a moment, she hesitated; her memory failed her in the matter. She paced along silently beneath the plane trees.

If naturalists were to be believed, the Great Silver Beetle was a noble creature, ethereal almost. She wondered if human relations would be any easier if the only indication of gender which we possessed was the shape of our feet. Life would be unquestionably duller. The whole Geoffrey affair might never have happened. Her feet had never been a strong point.

Bravely jerking herself out of thoughts about Geoffrey, she turned her mind to *Hygrobia hermanni*, the Screech Beetle, a very different kettle of fish. "It announces its presence by a loud squeak and a rubbing of its wings against the abdomen. It is a common species in muddy ponds."

Her thoughts turned, with what degree of consequence she was not sure, to her brother Jeremy. She had never encountered him in low dives or muddy ponds. But a rubbing of the wings against the abdomen would be a believeable activity in some of the friends that he had made for himself at Magdalen over the last three years, should they awake and find themselves beetles. Jeremy was naturally more gregarious than Evelyn. And she took it on trust that it takes all sorts to make a world. But much of the social life which agreed with her brother seemed to her incomprehensibly boring and pointless, a lot of standing about smoking in ill-ventilated rooms, chattering to nonentities. She felt that her father would hardly credit some of the things that were said on these occasions, nor some of the things that were smoked.

The Whirligig Beetles, *Gyrini natatores*, she recalled, swim about in crowds, in endless circles and gyrations on the surface of still water. How one distinguished their sex, she rather forgot.

Jeremy would probably grow up. She missed him, though. Since Geoffrey had come on the scene, and since Jeremy went to

Oxford, she had felt herself drifting apart from her brother. She did not know precisely who Jeremy's friends were; she merely had a sense that the boy had started to inhabit an effete and busy world which she could not penetrate. Nor had he ever cared for being spoken to as if he were a child by Geoffrey, who was, after all, only half a dozen years older than he was.

She walked a little further. Over her head, cumulo-nimbus clouds raced past, beyond the branches of a copper beech Geoffrey had said that her bush was copper-beech in colouring. It was, she supposed. He nuzzled about in it sometimes, like a monkey searching for fleas in its young. But nothing ever came of it.

It was odd, the way she remembered stray moments of sex like that, like flash-backs in a film.

Her thoughts passed from Whirligig Beetles to Great Diving Beetles; to *Ilybius ater*, the Mud-dwelling Beetle, about which she could remember nothing; until her mind finally rested in contemplation of *Platambus maculatus*, perhaps her favourite species, preferable even to the Great Silver Beetle, because less conspicuous.

"A handsome insect found mainly among submerged vegetation at the margins of running water," she said aloud, quoting from the public library book from which all this information was derived. And there her thoughts stopped.

She was the only person at the Round Pond. The harshness of the wind had driven away even the most hardened of nannies, pushing prams, or Spring Visitors looking for undesirable companionship. The trees were noisy and frenzied. Early blossoms flew about like confetti. Evelyn pulled her woollen hat more firmly on to her head and breathed hard into her mittens.

But it was as she turned back, down the path to the left of the Round Pond, that she realised that she was not alone in braving the weather. First, she saw some white envelopes scurrying down the path in front of her. And then, from behind, she heard a very foreign voice calling out, "Please! The letters! Please! If you would be so kind!"

Homo sapiens, male, aged, was her automatic reflection.

A stout old man, with a puce complexion and a white beard, ran along shouting. He waved a walking-stick in the air. But it looked more like a piece of decoration than something which he needed to help him get along.

Evelyn was naturally athletic. She ran after the letters and soon picked them up. Her mother's daughter, she instinctively looked at the names on the envelopes. One was addressed to a bank in St James's; one was marked *Air Mail* to a Swiss address; one, slightly startling, was addressed to a famous actor, who, although more or less retired, had recently made an impressive "come-back" in a part specially written for him in a new West End play.

Evelyn handed the envelopes back to their owner. Was he a man of the theatre? She thought that he probably was.

"Too kind," he said, collapsing on to a conveniently placed bench, which he tapped gently with his finger-tips, indicating that the girl was to sit beside him. She did so, telling herself that he was clearly a person with whom it was eminently safe to sit on a park bench in Kensington, and wondering at the same time if she believed it.

When she was close to him, she could see that there were very small veins all over his face; that what had looked like an even red from a distance was actually composed of many little rivers of blue and pink flowing beneath the surface of his cheeks. One of his eyes was rather bloodshot. He had a good head of hair, a thick white profusion, with no traces of baldness.

Puffing, a little exaggeratedly, he put a brown hat on his head and rubbed his cheeks with the palms of his hands. Evelyn was aware of the smell of moth-balls which appeared to be emanating from his expansive tweed trousers, whose creases hung loosely over highly-polished brown shoes like curtains sweeping a parquet floor.

She began to wonder if the old gentleman was going to have a heart attack; and, if people had heart attacks, what one did.

The occasional bird, pigeon or sparrow or starling – sometimes the first of the swifts and swallows — flew, or was blown past. Sometimes a Boeing 707, or an aeroplane so high in the clouds as to be unidentifiable, sent down its melancholy sigh through the winds.

"My hat!" the old gentleman suddenly exclaimed.

He had been unwise to put it on his head without holding it there. At first, Evelyn took his exclamation as metaphorical, but when she saw what had happened, she sprang to her feet and ran after it. Every time she stooped to pick it up, the wind tossed it a little further out of her reach, on to the lawn, up the slope, down the slope, until it found a resting place in a flower-bed. *Kerria japonica* and *prunus tenella* were almost in flower at the back of the border, shading irises and narcissi and late crocuses at the front. The hat was perched on the twiggy entrails of a thick, only slightly flowering forsythia bush. She grabbed it triumphantly and laughed.

The old gentleman on the bench was now some fifty yards away.

He had stood up and was shouting, "Excellent, excellent." His voice was absurdly loud, almost ludicrously foreign. She ran back.

Her face, slightly fey, had only the faintest touch of colour in its cheeks. Very red hair stuck out beneath a navy-blue woollen hat, of a shape and size then somewhat trendy. Her mouth was broad, and when she smiled as she did now, a lot of white teeth showed between her delicately curling lips. But it was with her eyes that she was smiling. She was rather tall, and as lithe as a boy.

"Here you are," she said, extending the hat to him, faintly with the tone of "and mind you look after it better in future."

"What a decrepit old fool I am; a worn-out old wind-bag," her companion protested. "Your excellent young legs, with the speed of Apollo, did what my worn-out stumps could never have done." There was an air of drama, combined with a hint of lechery, very faint, injected into his entire manner as he spoke — if *spoke* is not too mild a word to describe the way in which he seemed to declaim his words — which confirmed Evelyn's inkling

9

that he was an actor. But his face had a vaguely spiritual quality – something about the way in which the lips appeared to be constantly tasting something, and the eyes forever staring into the distance – which was powerfully alluring.

"Why should you run around parks in search of an Old Age Pensioner's belongings?"

"It was nothing, really." He half embarrassed, and half delighted her.

"My dear, you have a social conscience. You have retrieved an Old Age Pensioner's hat." This seemed to amuse him considerably. "I have fought against your country in a world war. But still they pay me a pension, and you retrieve my hat. You have rendered me an inestimable service. How to repay it? Perhaps you would permit me to repay you with tea, perhaps, and, perhaps, some cakes?"

This was an excellent idea, and it was pronounced in accents a good deal less foreign than those in which he had addressed her at first.

"I live in Pimlico," he said, as they turned for the Palace Gate. "It is too far, or I would invite you there. The hotel yonder does a very tolerable brew." He took evident pleasure in this idiomatic turn of phrase. They crossed Kensington Road, and, as they dodged the traffic, he took her arm.

The showy portals of the Earl of Oxford Hotel did not look very promising to Evelyn, who had very developed notions about what constituted "a good cup of tea". But, as they swung through the circular doors, it was suddenly warm and quiet. The carpet beneath her feet felt very soft. The old gentleman led the way – he was clearly familiar with the place – to a large "lounge" where they sat down in a corner in an expansive leather sofa. After the noises of wind and traffic, there was an almost eerie silence.

"Sit close to me; I am somewhat deaf," he said, almost sharply, "and if that young man will bring us some tea . . ."

A waiter appeared, as from nowhere. He asked what kind of tea they would like.

"China," said the old man, "with lemons and sugar."

"Strong Ceylon for me," said Evelyn firmly, "with milk. That is," her eyes faltered a little as she met her companion's gaze, "that is, if it is not too inconvenient."

"Not at all. I like people to be different. And a few cream cakes."

He seemed to exercise a spell over the waiter, who disappeared before Evelyn had time to mention toast.

There was a seemingly interminable silence, during which the old gentleman sat staring at the floor. Then he looked up, and announced, in a loud voice, "As you will come to realise, I am the most boring man in London; but worth meeting for that reason."

One or two people in the corners of the lounge laid down copies of *Country Life* and stared across at the performance which was being enacted on the sofa.

"Of course, Cedric Tomlinson *used* to be the most boring man in London," he added in tones of modesty. "But then, dear Cedric went and spoilt it all by writing a rather good book; and then, even less boring, by dying. You see, people can't keep it up. All the most interesting people are dead, of course. Death makes even the worst of bores interesting."

"What was the book about?" Death embarrassed her. She felt amused by a sort of Puckish charm in her companion, but irritated by the crudity with which he advertised himself. She saw force, for the first time, in Queen Victoria's distaste for being addressed as if she were a public meeting.

"What was Cedric's book about? Life!" The tone was dismissive. "A subject poor Cedric knew precious little about."

Evelyn had never heard of Cedric Tomlinson. She wondered whether she ought to have done. For an instant, she felt angered that the old gentleman had dropped a name without attempting to explain it. But actually, the instant past, she felt flattered. The mention of the name without explanation drew her into an assumed intimacy which made subsequent conversation easy.

"Do young people read Cedric's stuff now?"

"I don't think so. I'm a bad person to ask."

"You aren't a poetaster?"

"No."

"People of John Price's generation always found Cedric's verses somewhat hard to take seriously. For my part, I rather like

> We paced through all the vastness of the plain
> And saw the pity on the faces of the slain,
> Pity for those who slew and lived . . .

But it is not to your taste?"

"As I said, I'm not a good person to ask."

Tea, of two kinds, came. The waiter also brought a huge tray of sandwiches. Evelyn took a cucumber sandwich, but refused a cream horn. The old man took two cream horns and an egg sandwich.

They talked and talked.

"Cream horns are great tongue-looseners. People are always at their best after cream horns," he pontificated.

She sniggered.

"So, you read no verse. We are poles apart. You inhabit the world of prose and fact; I, the world of poetry and the imagination. A meeting of opposites, or a blending of perfect complements. Which is it to be? Crabbed age and youth . . ."

It was slightly disconcerting to find that, although his conversation consisted of almost entirely formulaic expressions of private fantasy, he actually appeared to have captured certain elements of her character with great perception.

She told him about her interest in beetles. He listened for a short while, and then, as if he had been silent for too long, he said, "But how do you come to be braving the elements in Kensington Gardens? It is a profound eccentricity which I should have allowed only to myself. I demand a history of your life and circle."

"Well, I'm a school-ma'am," she began. She talked about mathematics.

"And are you, like Melchizedek, without father or mother?"

"Lor, no. Pa's retired. They live in Bucks. Just out of Metroland."

She gave a run-down of her father's career; a number of important, but only faintly distinguished, jobs in the Diplomatic Corps, ending with an embassy in an African country recently granted independence.

Talk of her father led to an explanation of where she lived, a pretty mews flat off Exhibition Road, which was let to her at an absurdly low rent by a former colleague of her father's, Hugh Bennett, who was thought to be spending the next five years in New York at the United Nations.

"Ah!"

The old man sighed. There was silence, as if he had ceased, for a moment, to perform, and lapsed quietly into the seriousness of his own thoughts.

"You must know everyone in London," he said, resuming his former tone.

It was quite untrue. She had not minded until recently, but she winced slightly as he said it. Her circle was limited. She knew few people independently of Geoffrey. The affair had been so absorbing that she had rather let her other friendships slide. What independent friends she had were either contemporaries of her parents, or college friends from Cambridge days. For the past three years, she had spent almost every evening, and the occasional night, with Geoffrey; gone on holiday with Geoffrey; "gone out", walked out, as her mother would say, with Geoffrey. He had talked to her interminably about his own friends and circle. But few of them would want to keep up with her now that the affair was over. Once more, with what seemed like a shot in the dark, a wave of his wand of fantasy, the old gentleman had touched a raw nerve of truth.

"Everyone in London," he repeated in tones of barely disguised irony, giving a sweeping gesture with his arm, as if the air was dirty and he wanted to dust it. "Only flotsam and jetsam come my way in the wastes of Pimlico. But here, you are in the very centre of things."

She *was* lucky to have the flat. It was perfect; and she felt proud of the way she had added to its already pretty furnishings.

"But ah! How melancholy I feel when I hear of the useful lives of people like your father. Here I am, half in the grave — as you would say, with one foot firmly in the ground. And what have I done? All but nothing."

In spite of a number of leading questions of the sort which her mother would have produced at this juncture, Evelyn could not form much impression of how he spent or had spent his life. Had he been an actor? He laughed uproariously at this, and said that he had strutted and fretted his hour upon the stage but would soon be heard no more. Had he been a don? That was, he claimed, too grand a word. A writer? A poet? Who had not written something in their youth which they did not grow old enough to remember with shame? He, a poet? A mere ant on the foothills of Mount Parnassus.

Where did he come from? No, she did not mean Pimlico. True, true, here we have no abiding city. Had he been old enough, he would have fought against her country in the First War. She wondered whether she was mistaken, or whether, in an earlier part of the conversation, he had said that he *had* fought for the Germans . . .

His age was impossible to determine. His hair and beard were perfectly white, but his face, for all its veins, was not much wrinkled. He might not have been as old as sixty-five. She was no judge of such matters. Her father was seventy. Was this old gentleman as old as Pa? Put as baldly as that, the question seemed to have a kind of impropriety about it.

Outside, it was beginning to be dark. They must have been sitting together for two hours. The waiter was hovering near them once more.

"I regret to announce," said the old man, resuming the heaviest of German accents, "that I have no money about my person, and no cheque-book."

"How extraordinary," she said spontaneously, and not without what her mother would have called "edge". It seemed monstrous. She was still young enough to assume that the old always paid for the young on occasions of this kind. And it had been his suggestion that they should come to this grandiose hotel.

"Then, I suppose I had better pay," she said, chillily. She had been "conned".

Over a pound for tea. It was absurd. And he had had the cheek to eat two cream horns. Tea with Geoffrey, if taken at all, had been drunk out of mugs in her flat. She had not had hotel tea of this kind since her own schooldays, when her parents had taken her out for the weekend. If Evelyn had been asked to describe the taste of freedom, her palate would immediately supply cucumber sandwiches, eaten just before a return to dormitory prayers, and six more weeks of the terrible tyranny of her housemistress. Paying for such a taste seemed outrageous.

The waiter took away two pound notes and asked if there would be any change.

"I cannot apologise enough," said the old man. He was animated, as if, in a curious way, her pouting angry lips, her petulance, were exciting him. I only hope you will allow me to atone for my misdeeds by offering you luncheon tomorrow. This is my address, and, by way of introduction, my name."

He handed her a card from an elegant silver case, on which was printed in copperplate lettering, *Baron Dietrich Gormann: 98 Kempenfelt House, Fish Square, London.*

"There is something antiquated about still having cards, I know," he said with a smile. "But they have their uses."

"Well, Baron, my name is Evelyn Tradescant."

"*Enchanté.*" He clicked his heels with ludicrous politeness. "But please, I do not use my title. Plain Mr Gormann."

Evelyn wondered, if this was the case, why it was printed on the card.

"Can I expect you at my apartment then? Tomorrow? Some

time before twelve. I lunch early. Old-fashioned again, but there it is."

He was escorting her out of the hotel. As they emerged from the circular doors, he patted her gently on the buttocks and left his hand there for a while, sending a frisson, not undelightful, up her backbone.

"Tomorrow, then," he said.

"Well . . ."

But he had hailed a taxi, and climbed into it and was soon disappearing into the rush of Kensington Road; a bold gesture, she thought afterwards, for a man with no money in his pocket.

2

She was more or less obliged to go to luncheon the next day. She
wanted, in some ways, to wound him by not going. But another
part of her demanded its rights and wanted to be repaid for the tea.
She did not know what was to guarantee that she would not be
swindled into paying for the lunch as well. And she did not want
to miss her walk in the Gardens and get behind with her beetles.
She had been considering going on to snails for some time already.

She knew, nevertheless, that she would go. She had not had a
luncheon date for ages, still less one with a baron. And a German
baron, too.

Snobs, like Geoffrey, would point out that the foreign aristocracy are not "the real thing". They missed the point that this is
precisely why such people are fascinating. For all one knew, they
might be complete frauds, not aristocrats at all. On the other hand,
their titles might be as old as Charlemagne. One felt, what one
would be unlikely to feel in many of England's great houses,
unsafe in their presence.

But "Mr Gormann" had touched deeper nerves in Evelyn than
those of social adventure.

She soaped and bathed herself that morning with particular
thoroughness.

She was unable to tell herself why it should be so, but she felt that her life was entering a new phase, a phase of which Mr Gormann was the herald. It was a little like the first time she had ever worn make-up, a habit long since abandoned. Her mother and father had been out, and she had gone into the bedroom to plunder the dressing-table. As she had painted her eyes and nails and lips – she was about ten at the time – she felt herself changing. She decided, in the instant, that she would refuse to go to any more children's parties; that she would no longer consent to have a bath with Jeremy; and she would not wear Alice bands any more, either. In her body, inexplicable sensations warned her that she had turned into a different person.

More obviously analogous to the present moment, was when she heard from her housemistress that she had won her scholarship to Newnham. Miss Harker had squeezed her. It was a gesture of congratulation reserved only for "gels", as she termed them, who won scholarships to the more ancient seats of learning. Those who won exhibitions were merely shaken by the hand. Since she had become a teacher herself, Evelyn had met many people to annoy and dismay her, but no one in the category of Miss Harker, a plump embodiment, it now seemed, of the competitive principle in education. But, even as her cheek rested on the buttons and bosom of this distinguished woman, Evelyn had felt an enormous sense of release and liberty. Again, she thought of the things which she would no longer have to do: never sleep in a dormitory, or wear a gym tunic or go to Communion.

As life turned out, these premonitions were chiefly accurate. Now, unmistakable and thrilling, the feeling of transition from an old life to a new, as she had experienced it in Miss Harker's arms, came over her as she lay in her bath and thought of Mr Gormann.

She wondered why tea with a strange old gentleman should have occasioned this reaction. It was not that she regarded him as a substitute for Geoffrey. She felt determined never to make "that" mistake again. She hardly knew the old gentleman; still less could she be said to love him. But she already felt that he was beginning to charm her life. In a way that it was impossible to articulate, she knew that it no longer mattered that everything had turned out so messily with Geoffrey.

The truth was, that she was no longer lonely.

As she padded out, wrapped in an enormous bath-towel to warm herself by the gas fire in the sitting room, she debated with herself whether to wear a skirt for such a luncheon. She decided, on the whole, against it. She was obliged to wear a skirt for teaching, and she enjoyed spending as much of the holiday as she could in trousers. Black velvet trousers and a white blouse would be smart enough for this occasion. One did not want to be over-dressed. She had even worn that outfit at a dinner party before now. If it were not centrally heated in Fish Square, she could wear a leather jerkin over her blouse. After a moment's consideration of brooches, she decided to wear a pendant Celtic cross around her neck.

She sat for a long time before the fire, and then she arrayed herself in a dark blue tweed suit, dark tights and sensible shoes. On the collar of her jacket, she wore a brooch that her mother had bought her to wear for her Degree ceremony. When she was done, what she saw in the glass gave distinct pleasure.

It was much warmer today. The wind had dropped, and sun shone on the Exhibition Road. She hardly needed her woollen hat and mittens. There was a bounce in her walk as she went down to South Kensington Station.

Pink, recently cleaned, the Natural History Museum stood out against a blue sky like a Romanesque cathedral converted for temporary use into a town hall.

She bought a ticket for as far as Victoria. There was no point in going all the way to Pimlico and changing trains on a nice day like this. She would walk when she got to Victoria.

Evelyn had never been to Fish Square before; she had not even heard of it. She half imagined a rococo *Schloss*, set back from pools where dolphins gambolled with mermaids and sea-horses. The thought, unusually fanciful for her, came as a surprise. But she could not begin to reconstruct a suitable setting for the conversations of the sort she had had the day before, without letting her mind drift off into fantasy.

Twenty minutes later, she emerged into the sunshine at Victoria and tripped gaily into the Vauxhall Bridge Road. It was a thoroughfare where she had frequently caught buses – Geoffrey had, for a time, affected rooms on the edges of Lambeth – but she had never walked down the length of it. It was wide, remote and seemingly endless; something like roads in dreams in which she found herself walking but making no discernible progress. The images for this nightmare must have been drawn from American films; and indeed, it was some surprise that the traffic meandering up and down the road was so obviously British: Fiats, Volkswagens in endless queues behind French lorries.

She passed the odd shop. They looked shabby, as if they might receive stolen property, but had not been open since 1948. As one approached the river, the wind got up. Newspapers stained with grease and vinegar blew about vindictively, clinging to her ankles. The buildings became larger on either side of the road – warehouses, factories, churches; lumps of dark red against the sky. Evelyn would have thought it certain that she had mistaken her turning if there had been any noticeable turning to mistake.

But, as if to pacify her fears, the buildings began to wear an occupied look again; curtains appeared in windows as she passed. Domestic-looking doors, freshly painted, decorated by the occasional burglar alarm, appeared to left and right. Shops once more appeared respectable and middle-class. Suddenly, the river was in sight. Spacious, gracious Bessborough Gardens spread themselves out before her.

She stood on the kerb by some traffic lights. She had been growing frightened. London was still capable of scaring her, in the ruthless way that it plunged one into areas totally hostile and unrecognisable. The comfortable sight of Pimlico made her heartbeat less urgent.

She approached a black policeman and asked the way to Fish

Square. He indicated a huge façade, overlooking the river. It had the air of having been modern in the late thirties. Now, it seemed simply big; something between a colossal office-block and a hospital. It was not a square at all; it was a cube.

The whole of a block, from street-corner to street-corner, was taken up with this solid complex of buildings. There were a number of different entrances, all barred by automatic traffic barriers, horizontal barbers' poles with prickles all over them. At the front, and in the very centre, a neon sign advertised the presence of a restaurant and a sports club. Other entrances bore the names of famous admirals; there was a Drake, a Rodney, an Anson, an Effingham, and so on. Kempenfelt House, her destination, looked exactly like all the others.

Inside, it was rather like an hotel. She walked through glass doors to a reception desk, where she was questioned by a middle-aged woman dressed like an air-hostess.

Miss Tradescant? Mr Gormann was expecting her. Apartment ninety-eight was on the third floor.

Carpeted corridors, all blue and decorated with fish, led off in every direction to doors with numbers on them. There were no windows in the corridors, so that, however high one rose in the building, it felt subterranean.

It was the perfect setting for a life of total anonymity. But Evelyn found it somewhat comic that a man who claimed to inhabit a world of poetry should have elected to live in such a place. She, on the other hand, who happily confessed to living in the world of prose, had her pretty mews flat; the Park no distance away in one direction; the Victoria and Albert Museum, Harrods, the Brompton Oratory, equally near in the other. She was surrounded, as Geoffrey had so often remarked, by temples of the sheerest fantasy. Perhaps that is why I do not need poetry — all that quotation and name-dropping, she thought, as the lift doors opened and she emerged on to the third floor.

"An Old Age Pensioner hobbles to greet you. Welcome, welcome!" He was coming down the carpet towards her. "Fiona downstairs rang to say you'd arrived. Come inside."

His flat was not particularly spacious; nor particularly elegant. But it was comfortable, and it contained what looked to Evelyn's eye like distinctively German objects, knobbly clocks and decorated pipe-racks being the sort of thing to catch the eye. Some delicate china figurines were kept in a glass case near the writing-table. Portraits of severe-looking men and women adorned the walls. Outside the window, most surprisingly, one saw London again in the sunshine; a picture-postcard view of the Thames and the Palace of Westminster.

"It is an odd kind of existence as you can see," said Mr Gormann. "But it is highly convenient. They are all service flats. If you knew my trouble with housekeepers . . ."

Evelyn responded with a nod. She was very nervous, wondering if they could carry off a luncheon *tête-à-tête* after so short an acquaintance.

If Mr Gormann was similarly apprehensive, he was better at concealing the fact. He looked more spruce than on the previous day. He wore a white shirt, which made his face seem even ruddier, a blue spotted bow tie, and a double-breasted dark blue suit. So, they were both in the same colour. As he moved about the room preparing drinks, Evelyn was struck by the lightness of his steps. It was as if his hefty-looking body had no weight at all.

"You will have a little Campari and soda? An extravagant habit of mine; but I find that luncheon does not come easily to me if I omit it."

She murmured something about that being lovely.

"A habit which I acquired in Geneva long, long ago," he continued.

He dispensed the drinks. He had obviously decided to satisfy her curiosity about himself by telling her some carefully selected detail about his past.

"What did you do in Geneva?" asked Evelyn after a longish pause.

"Ah, it is funny that you should ask that. It was your own

22

father's career which made me think about it all again. I was working for the League of Nations. But that was a thousand years ago. You have not even heard of the League of Nations."

"Oh, I have; just about."

"Just about. How humbling it is to be made aware of one's obsolescence." He stroked his beard, smiling. Did he, she wondered, deliberately miss her tone?

"We all felt so passionately about the League at the time. Even the young Gormann. He was not totally unintelligent, I suppose. But it did not fully dawn on him until 1936 what was happening to his country. Thank God it was not later. He had time and money. He settled in Zurich and became a Swiss citizen. His father had always banked in Switzerland, so there was not much difficulty about transferring."

"Weren't you sad to leave at all?" asked Evelyn, examining his face intently, and trying to tell whether he was Jewish.

"One was naturally sad to leave Germany. You British laughed at us for calling it the Fatherland. It was naturally sad to leave the house where I had been brought up; where I had made most of my friends, read most of my favourite books for the first time . . ."

"Did you sell it?"

"How could I sell it? Nobody had any money to buy a place of that size. They took it. I have never been back."

"The Nazis?"

"People always think of the Nazis. Now, why should an old man bore you with this ancient history?"

"So you are still Swiss?"

"I spend a few months in Zurich each year as a general rule." His shrug suggested a mild resentment at being bullied with questions to which he had not specifically rehearsed the answer. "Let us go downstairs for lunch."

They came out of the lift in a part of the building which was identical to all that Evelyn had seen, except for the fact that the carpets were red, and not blue.

"The little restaurant here is rather pedestrian, I fear," said Mr

Gormann, "and the décor is dispiriting. But we shall manage somehow."

He led the way into a dark blue room where revolving pale blue electric lights gave one the impression of being under water. As they sat down at the table, Evelyn realised that part of the restaurant really was under water, water in which young men and women were swimming about. She thought how inelegantly their equipment, snorkels and the like, compared with the similar apparatus hawked around by beetles.

"Richard Evans and David often come to bathe there." said Mr Gormann. "You see, the swimming-pool is built on a slightly higher level than the restaurant, so we can look through a glass wall and see under the water. Grander than tropical fish, in a way. You must come one day, since you are fond of swimming."

"I should love to."

It was beginning to dawn on Evelyn that the old gentleman was rich. The effect of the realisation was striking. She felt herself becoming quite stiff and breathless with excitement. Yesterday, there had been indications of what her mother would have called "being comfortable" about the old man's appearance. His shoes, for instance, were evidently costly. But now, looking across the table, she felt sure that he was more than comfortable. His pink, stubby fingers, soft and well manicured, were holding a menu. They alone seemed to confirm her suspicions. Wealth gives off its own intangible feel – odour, almost, lending credence to the expression, "stinking rich".

"There are a lot of things here which are not worth eating," he said, handing the menu across to her. "I have Sole *Bonne Femme* every day. It saves the bother of having to make a decision. Besides, fish suits Gormann. But don't let that limit you."

Evelyn said that she would have the same.

The restaurant was what Geoffrey would have called "too, too, ghastly". Actually, Evelyn thought that it was rather jolly to be so submarine and fishy, and she said so elaborating, as she had done, yesterday, on her fondness for Natural History. Mr Gormann seemed quietly amused.

As she spoke, looking through the blue light at his grey beard, she thought of the Great Silver Beetle, found mainly among submerged vegetation at the margins of running water.

Lesser species pecked at their food in different corners of the restaurant. Evelyn and Mr Gormann drank a bottle of hock which seemed to go down very easily.

She wondered if she was going to hear any more about his past, but nothing was volunteered. The possibility occurred to her that she had offended him; been too prying; asked the wrong sort of question. But he seemed so amiable and unruffled that a much likelier explanation was that he had said all that he had decided it was necessary to say on that occasion.

As they were drinking their coffee, Mr Gormann leant forward and looked into Evelyn's eyes with an almost hypnotic stare.

"You know, by a remarkable coincidence, I was speaking to John Price on the telephone last night. You know one another, I gather. It confirms my suspicion that you know everyone in London."

She was startled. Perhaps she was a bit drunk. She did recall that he had mentioned the name of John Price, in connection with the poet, Cedric Tomlinson. But Price is a common enough name, and she had not made the connection with a friend, often mentioned by Geoffrey, whom she had met once or twice since arriving in London.

It embarrassed her that she had still not entirely escaped Geoffrey's orbit. Lunch with a stray old gentleman met in a park seemed an adventurous way of escaping from her former attachment. But the escape was evidently not to be complete.

"Quite an admirer of yours," Mr Gormann was saying.

"Who?"

"Why, John Price."

"But, I . . . we have only met very, very briefly. I can't have seen him for at least a year."

"He remembers you and admires you." The old gentleman's

25

persistence with the subject was tedious.

"Pimlico" Price; why so called, she never found out. As far as she could summon an image of him to mind, she did not think that his admiration of her was reciprocated. He was a big, rather plummy-voiced man, in her recollection, about ten years older than Geoffrey. He did something in the City, and had estates in Scotland. On the only occasion when she had ever spoken to him at length, he had been giving an uninspiring account of the workings of one of the old city companies – Haberdashers, Merchant Taylors, Coppersmiths, she forgot which. He was in a white tie and tails at about six in the evening and just off to one of their banquets. He had popped in to a party which she and Geoffrey once gave in her flat.

Actually, she had first heard of Pimlico Price a year or so before she met Geoffrey. Said to have something of a taste for women, and young women at that, his name had been mentioned in connection with Tansy Bonchurch's sister Laura. Pimlico Price was one of those remote beings from the outside world who haunted undergraduate parties at Cambridge. She had heard his voice imitated a good deal. "That's a nice pair of titties" was a phrase often rendered in a Pimlico manner, and it did little to attract her to him. It was striking to hear his name mentioned again, in this very different context.

She wondered how much Pimlico Price had known about her and Geoffrey. Geoffrey was always very discreet, a precaution with which she was emotionally much in sympathy. They hardly ever held hands in public, for example. The erotic aspects of their relationship had been conducted in the completest privacy, and they seemed to have no bearing on the way they spent the rest of their time. Geoffrey never led up to sexual encounters.

It was therefore perfectly possible that Pimlico knew nothing of the affair. Now, their frantic secrecy about it seemed odd. At the time, it was because she did not want her parents to know. Perhaps Price thought she and Geoffrey were "just good friends". But she did remember hearing Pimlico once described as "a fearful

26

gossip". There was even talk of his having been held back in his career in the City because of congenital habits of indiscretion.

"I do not know how well you know John," Mr Gormann was saying, "but I am distinctly worried about him. He seems to have no settled plan for the future. In some ways, he is very well established, of course. But his work is very boring. He is a drifter. I fear that this is the inevitable consequence of having rather too much money and almost no interests in life. Of course, the present financial crises are worrying and demoralising for all of us. They worry old Gormann. But, I don't know. John seems positively eaten up by them."

"I do not know Mr Price at all well."

"Precisely. That is one of the very points about him which worry me. Who does know John well? None of us do. He needs some solid, binding human tie before it is too late."

"I'm not sure I think it's necessarily a good thing to tie yourself down. The only good thing about some human relationships is that they are not lasting."

"No wonder John speaks so highly of you, if you profess such cynical views to him."

They should not have drunk so much hock in the middle of the day. The conversation took a strangely intimate turn, hovering around Mr Gormann's feelings for Price and Evelyn's views on what other people called love.

She did not actually mention Geoffrey by name, or allude to the affair. But it was obvious, as she spoke, that she was discussing her own experiences.

There had been undergraduates at Newnham who had been rather keen on rabbiting on about "relationships"; and, of course, it was her mother's life blood. But she had never gone in for it until now. The wine, and the fact that the old man was still a stranger to her, combined with the extraordinary fact that he believed that Price had been admiring her from afar to make the conversation wildly exhilarating.

"Come upstairs for some tea," said Mr Gormann, having paid

the enormous bill for lunch. No allusion was made to yesterday, and the tea for which she had paid. Three hours had passed without her noticing, and it was tea-time again.

She protested, lamely, for form's sake; suggested that there was reason for her rushing away; acquiesced in the idea of a "quick cup", and said that she did not in the least mind what sort it was.

As they drank Lapsang together upstairs, they began to talk to each other in a new tone, as if they were intimates, with shared experience and a shared view of things. It was hard to know how such a thing could have happened after a single lunch. There was so much that neither knew about the other; and Evelyn felt, her head mildly spinning, events were moving at such a pace that there were things which neither of them would ever stop to find out.

Gyrini natatores, Whirligig Beetles: they swim about in endless circles and gyrations.

It was half past five, and becoming cold again, when she finally parted from the old man. A pat on the bottom was his only valediction.

3

It was only when she told him that she was going to see her parents that she realised how far things had gone. She discovered that it was necessary to apologise. Her father had a recent birthday; she wanted to see her brother before the Oxford term began; and so on. She had found it necessary in her life to give such accounts of herself to no one before — unless to her parents themselves, when, having promised them that she would come home on a particular date, more attractive possibilities, social or amatory, had presented themselves. Even Geoffrey, in the days when he had been most demanding, had not awakened in her the feeling that time not spent with him must be accounted for.

"You will be away, exactly, how long?"

"Just till Sunday."

"But you are *leaving* on Friday afternoon," Mr Gormann said, as if it were a shameful detail, which, though already confessed, had been slurred over and not given due emphasis. Heavy irony had then been adopted.

"Your parents doubtless have greater claims on you than I do. A lonely Old Age Pensioner will spend a solitary Saturday afternoon."

It was absurd. He had other friends. And there was the campaign to save Chelsea to be getting on with. But he had made her feel guilty, laughing down the telephone a desperate sort of laugh.

"It won't be long."

"When you are young, your time-scale is different, my dear. If you had let me know sooner that you were going I could have escorted you to the station. Goodbye."

He had hung up at once.

She wondered how she could have allowed the whole thing to happen. Old people, she knew, were frequently possessive. But to have convinced her that he was entitled to be as possessive as that was skilful beyond the average.

Certainly, they got along together very well; they enjoyed one another's talk. And this was in itself remarkable, given the randomness of their first encounter. They did not have much in common in the usual sense. But conversation was easy between them. He made subjects which she had formerly found dull come alive with personal anecdote. Politics, for instance, fascinated him. He had known Mosley when the latter was still a Labour MP, and, while professing distaste for the later developments of that career, he had a lot of interesting memories of the man and his circle. He talked, too, of names less familiar to her, associated with the League; or of his eight years in Heidelburg; or of his father's career in the army.

Names, too, from his immediate circle in London frequently cropped up. But, in spite of the coincidence of being vaguely acquainted with some of them — most notably with Pimlico Price — he never suggested that she should meet any of his friends. On the only occasion when she had asked him to supper with two old Newnhamite friends of hers — now civil servants — he had pleaded tiredness as an excuse and failed to appear.

She sympathised with his desire to keep his friends in separate compartments, while being mildly irritated by it. He frequently admitted that he had discussed her with John Price, always repeating that this person was "quite an admirer" of hers. But the admiration was never to be allowed, it seemed, any practical expression.

Though tiresome, disconcerting even, being talked about was a kind of flattery; not the only kind, she recognised, that Mr Gormann had used to make the last few weeks pass so pleasantly. Perpetual admiration was what one missed most when a love affair had gone wrong, and Mr Gormann filled the gap left by Geoffrey in a way that was inevitably exhilarating, since he seemed to show no signs of becoming her lover. He wanted her *for what she was*, she told herself, confidently drawing an old-fashioned distinction between herself and her sexual organs. Certainly, anyway in latter days, Geoffrey had been no great shakes in that direction. If she felt frustrated now, it was less embarrassing than feeling so when Geoffrey was lying on top of her, reaching hasty little climaxes and flopping back exhausted before she had begun to be interested.

She enjoyed her weekend, in spite of its awkward moments. Her parents fussed inordinately about Jeremy in a way that they had never done for her. When she arrived, they were barely able to suppress their anxiety enough to give her a civil greeting. Jeremy had gone out three hours earlier on his motor-bike and not returned. Anything, as her father kept repeating, could have happened to the boy. Lady Tradescant's benign reassurance, every time her husband made this assertion of the infinite unpredictability of events, that Jeremy had no idea of time, was small comfort. She evidently betrayed an equal inability to think of anything but their son's fate, in spite of the calm way in which she turned the pages of a novel by Georgette Heyer.

Although irritated by her parents, Evelyn no longer quarrelled with them; and her filial devotion was sincere. She sat in silence with them as they crossed their legs and looked at their watches. It was sad to see them growing old. Sir Derek's hair, which had been silvery when he left his last embassy six years before, was now a whitish yellow, and much thinner. His mandarin eyes, concealed behind steel-rimmed spectacles, saw less than they used to; and arthritis was making him stoop noticeably. His wife was still after a fashion, a fashion that passed away soon after Munich, pretty; but

the lines around her mouth were becoming more fixed and pronounced. She was fifteen years younger than Sir Derek; but now
he was past seventy. Since the publication of *Neither One Thing nor
the Other: An Ambassador's Reflections*, life had been uneventful,
centring round gardening, church and the family. His book had
not sold at all well.

Lady Tradescant's family was extensive – she was a Judd – and
the contemplation of the courtship, marriages, births and demises
of her siblings and their children provided all the occupation
which her mind required. Sir Derek, who did not share her
interest, and had no memory for names – a disability which had pre-
cipitated more than one diplomatic awkwardness – was
languishing into boredom as his retirement progressed.

An adoration of Jeremy, by no means a child of their youth, was
the most consistent unifying force between them, as Evelyn saw it.
Sir Derek had high ambitions for the boy, hoping, in spite of a
singular lack of interest on Jeremy's part, that his son would follow
him into the Foreign Office. Since the first dawning of Jeremy's
manhood, before "O" Levels, Sir Derek had demonstrated undis-
guisedly his passion that the boy should be a success. In this, he
showed an aggressiveness absent in his dealings with almost everyone else. His nickname among Embassy staff of "Limp" Tradescant had not been chosen for nothing. But it fascinated Evelyn,
while she was still an undergraduate, to see the almost firm look
about her father's lips when reading Jeremy's school reports.

"What do you suppose your housemaster means by 'lacka-
daisical'?" he would snap down the breakfast table.

"That's the Judd in you, darling, I'm afraid. But it's nice that
you're coming on so well with the clarinet." Lady Tradescant's
efforts to reassure – Evelyn thought of them now as they sat waiting for Jeremy to appear on his motor-bike – had a frequently
upsetting effect.

Whatever the housemaster had meant, drugs had sometimes
been mentioned during Jeremy's schooldays, although nothing
concrete ever came to light. Failing – inexplicably to Sir Derek's

mind – to offer Jeremy an award, his Oxford college had offered him a place as a commoner, and he was now in his final year there reading history.

Evelyn felt that her mother was much better equipped to understand Jeremy than his father ever was. Whether or not more a Judd than a Tradescant, Jeremy had one simple feature in common with his mother: good looks. Evelyn, who had not felt the need to compete with her brother in this respect, recognised him as dazzlingly better-looking than herself. She had no reason to be jealous. She innocently delighted in his appearance. Her mother, she felt, being a mother, and more than usually handsome herself, was granted an insight about the boy markedly lacking in Sir Derek. Lady Tradescant knew the perils of the course, the dangers involved in being beautiful, in a way that Evelyn was frank enough to acknowledge that she and her father did not.

Needless to say, Jeremy eventually turned up, though not until the tea had stood cold and undrunk in his father's cup for three-quarters of an hour.

"You *hitch-hiked?*" they heard Lady Tradescant saying to him at the kitchen door.

Sir Derek leapt from the table.

"Has there been an accident? Why on earth didn't you ring us up?"

Jeremy emerged into the dining-room – they still had tea at the table, a relic of nursery days – his cheeks flushed with fresh air. His hair was a little longer than when Evelyn had last seen him, but not long by present standards. It was the only hair which she had ever seen that was really golden, not merely yellow or fair. It just covered the tops of his ears, in almost crisp curls, like a classical statue come to life. He was encumbered with motor-cycling para-phernalia, which suited him: a black leather jacket, zipped up to the neck, jeans, boots laced up to his knees. He carried a scarlet helmet under one arm. Soft, rather sensuous lips and enormous eyes formed an ingenuous smile, as he looked about him at their worried, slightly angry faces.

"There's no need to make such a fuss, Pa, really.'

"But what do you mean by engine-trouble?"

"How am I to know?"

"Who gave you a lift?"

"A guy in a lorry."

"You mean a lorry-driver."

"A guy in a lorry. A lorry-driver. What difference does it make?"

"Your mother was worried. You should take more care. How many times have I told you not to accept lifts?"

"Never."

"Well, common sense should tell you."

The three of them settled down to an impenetrable quarrel, while Evelyn went to the drawing-room to read Darwin. She read his reflections on the parentage of domestic pigeons. "No amount of crossing between only six or seven wild forms could produce races so distinct as Pouters, Carriers, Runts, Fantails, Turbits, Short-faced Tumblers, Jacobins and Trumpeters. How could crossing produce, for instance, a Pouter and a Fantail, unless the supposed aboriginal parents possessed the remarkable characters of these breeds?" She admired what she read, and looking up towards the hall, where the argument was still in progress, she thought Darwin wise.

But it did not take long for the quarrel to subside. Sir Derek went into the study to listen to the wireless — what he called thinking things out — while his children caught up with family news, imparted by their mother in the drawing-room.

"Alix has had a baby — Gwen rang the other day — and apparently he is simply *gorgeous*. They've decided to call him Gabriel — but then, they say a lot of these names are coming back."

They heard in some detail about Alix's confinement, punctuating their mother's talk with appropriate comments from time to time. Evelyn felt happy. Jeremy was more at ease too, his father being out of the room. The subject of Alix exhausted, they passed to Julia's marriage, thought to be on the rocks; her younger brother Tim, who had just passed Common Entrance, to become the umpteenth Judd at Marlborough; old Harvey, getting better from his stroke, but what could you expect at eighty? Margaret, whose holiday in Southern Italy had been a simply huge success. They nodded appreciatively. Seemingly inane, Lady Tradescant had a wisdom as deep as instinct. Neither of her children shared her interest in the Judds and their doings, but no subject could have been better chosen to make them forget the hitch-hiking controversy.

The telephone, ringing in the hall, interrupted them.

"Presumably for me," said Jeremy, stubbing a cigarette out into a flower-vase as he went to the door.

"I wish he wouldn't smoke," sighed his mother; and she added, as if to explain the telephone call, "he leads such a gay life."

Evelyn raised her eyebrows.

"I expect it's that Jennifer he was so fond of last term," Lady Tradescant continued.

"What's she like?"

"Your father knew *her* father during the war and thinks he was not quite the thing. But she's a nice girl. And simply dotty on Jeremy."

"Is he fond of her?"

"We don't *ask*." A coy laugh, accompanied by a little shrug implied that Jeremy was too much a one for the ladies for such a question to have been sensible. The girl-friend had been mentioned before on earlier visits home, but Evelyn had never heard anything of her from Jeremy himself. She was aware, whenever the subject came up, of sensations of simple jealousy, too strong to make her mother's observations on the matter tolerable. She was aware of Lady Tradescant's desire to marry both her children "suitably", and to have grandchildren. In her own case, she was so embarrassed by the prospect as to be able to dismiss it from consideration altogether. But she thought of herself in some senses as a co-guardian, with her mother, of Jeremy's destiny, and the airy way in which Lady Tradescant gave voice to her ambitions on his behalf brought an irrational and protective anger close to the surface.

The boy returned with a faintly startled expression on his face.

"It's for you, sis," he said.

Her father was leaving the study, almost too casually, as she came out into the hall. He lingered a few moments before entering the drawing-room, so as to catch the opening words of her conversation.

Stupidly, she had no notion of who it might be. She was surprised to hear Mr Gormann's voice when she picked up the receiver.

"I was anxious, dear girl. How was your journey?"

"No need to be anxious. It isn't a long journey, you know."

"Is that so? You must pardon Gormann's complete ignorance of geography — and his idiotic tendency to panic. I felt sure that something might have happened to you."

"Nothing has happened to me." It was the truth. She was cross with him for making this intrusion into her home. Her parents, perhaps, were telling Jeremy about her "boy-friends" and speculating about which one this would be. There would be questions, implied or explicit, at the supper table.

"You matter too much to me — which is why I worry."

"Yes." A click on the line informed her that Lady Tradescant was already upstairs, listening in on the extension in her bedroom.

"I meant to ask you — but you flew away so suddenly — if you could manage supper with me on Sunday night."

"But it's all arranged. You did ask me."

She had half a mind to cancel it, she felt so cross.

"Sheer senility, dear girl. And did I ask you if our homely restaurant here would be in the least possible?"

"Lovely. Look, I'm perfectly all right. I'll see you on Sunday."

"You are eating. You are in the middle of a meal?"

"No. It's only six o'clock."

"I have the most tiresome habit of ringing people up when they are eating. Senility, pure senility. Our mutual friend says that he

36

has only to ladle soup into a plate to make his telephone ring and my voice appear at the other end of it."

"Our mutual friend?"

"John Price. He has just been with me now, as a matter of fact. He was telling me more about the wonderful party that he once attended in your flat."

"*That* again." She was amused, pleased.

"So blasé. As if wonderful parties were a part of daily life. Of course, for you, I dare say that they are. Poor John. I am trying to make him *relax* more. I've never known a man who expended so much energy so needlessly. You must throw another wonderful party and invite him to it. He is longing to meet you again."

"I can't think why."

"You are much sought after. I've told him that I shan't forgive him if he steals you from me." The joking, bantering tone was heavy.

"He is too much involved in our so-called crisis. He lives too close to the heart of things in Threadneedle Street. Ancients like Gormann know what a real financial crisis is like. When you see whole currencies collapse."

"Mm. Have you been for your walk today, or have you been slacking? I can't trust you once my back is turned."

Unconscious, gradually, of her mother listening to the conversation, Evelyn allowed it to dawdle flirtatiously on for about half an hour. Mr Gormann described a lunch he had been to, with a blow by blow account of every course. At last, he said, "My dear, I'm keeping you from your delightful family."

"Not at all." The telephone clicked. In a moment, Lady Tradescant was ostentatiously flushing a lavatory.

"I miss you, dear girl. *À dimanche*."

"*À dimanche*."

She put the receiver down. She decided to say nothing to her parents about the call. For once, they must mind their own business, and she would brave out their silent curiosity. There would be too much explaining to do, of a kind which she felt not merely unwilling but unable to provide. Sir Derek, surely, would not appreciate the notion of his daughter making friends with old men picked up in public parks. Lady Tradescant would worry about Mr Gormann's age; more bluntly, his capacity for providing her with grandchildren. Evelyn knew that she would be unable to tell them, moreover, many *facts* about Mr Gormann; who he really was, how he spent his time when he was not with her; who, apart from the enigmatic Pimlico Price, his friends were; or how he could be rich and indolent enough to live in Fish Square.

Blushing, she returned to the drawing-room.

Jeremy was leaning against the mantelpiece smoking a cigarette. She noticed what very protruding buttocks he had, a feature emphasised by his denim cycling-trousers.

"Fancy your knowing old Theo," he said.

"Theo who?" asked Sir Derek.

"Theo Gormann."

"Theo Gormann the drama critic?" asked his father cautiously.

"Oh, that phase," said the boy knowingly, letting smoke out through his nostrils.

"I never had any time for the man. A complete charlatan," said Sir Derek in his cross voice. "I'm sorry to think of you mixing with people of that kind."

"Who's this, darling?" said Lady Tradescant, coming back into the room and pushing her hair into place with the palms of her hands.

"Theo Gormann."

"Wasn't he that Blackshirt who was such a friend of Goebbels?" she asked innocently.

Jeremy giggled.

"Nothing was ever made clear about that. We must be exceedingly careful what we say." An official tone crept into Sir Derek's voice. "Good heavens, we could have the Official Secrets Act and the law of libel and I don't know what coming down on our heads if we weren't careful."

It seemed an unlikely possibility in the quietness of their own drawing-room.

"I must be mixing him up with someone else," said Lady Tradescant.

Evelyn, feeling as out of things as she had done during the quarrel about the motor-bike, stood in blank silence while her family engaged in this series of exchanges. Her parents, and her brother, too, had encountered her secret friend, and appeared to know more biographical details about him than she did herself. It was so astonishing that she felt dizzy, unable to know, should they ask her, what she would say. But they had not finished.

"Actually, it's just absurd to talk about Theo being a Nazi." Jeremy, shaken into seriousness, was smoking vigorously. "Just because a guy's a German, people go bandying around . . ."

"I think I know more about that than you do, if I may say so."

"I thought he *was* that awful man who pretended to be a pacifist and then sold arms to Hitler. But that was ages ago." Lady Tradescant's voice trailed off pleasantly. Faintly annoyed to be interrupted, her husband continued:

"There was some talk of the kind – but one should be very careful what one says. His brother was the director of a munitions factory in Koblenz, as a matter of fact. It was never actually proven that even he had Nazi leanings, let alone Gormann himself, who left Germany three years before the outbreak of war."

"I could have sworn Dr Goebbels came into it somewhere. Horrible man. He of course was the real *brains* behind the whole thing. Worse than Hitler, really." She turned to Jeremy to explain, in the kindly voice one might use when telling a child about sex; only in this case the particular matter discussed, brains, being infinitely less desirable and more dangerous.

"The pacifism," Sir Derek continued, "was, as far as one could make out, genuine. Ban the Bomb was the last thing I'd heard of his being mixed up in. I'm afraid I always thought he was rather an exhibitionist."

"Hardly the same thing as being a Nazi," said Jeremy, who did not appear to have been following what his father said, but speaking in tones as if he had won a point in an argument.

"Anyway," his father had said, "I should never have thought of him cropping up again after all this time. As a matter of fact, I thought he would have . . . er . . ." He seemed to be seeking for an appropriately mild synonym for "dead", but, being unable to do so, left the sentence in mid air.

"I don't suppose he's really a *friend* of Evelyn's," said her mother, unwisely, trying to draw her into the conversation.

"I should hope not."

"Not particularly."

They could tell from the stubborn way in which she shut her lips that it would be useless to press for an explanation then and there. Families, like the Nazis, have ways of making us talk. But it takes time.

Evelyn braved it out, and said nothing. In spite of the awkwardness, she had a happy two days. Home was comfortable. Eighteenth-century brick set back among lawns gave one the illusion of refuge and rest.

As she sat in the train on Sunday evening, watching Metroland flash past, Evelyn rather wished that she had had the chance to talk about Mr Gormann with Jeremy. It was not, once she thought about it, surprising, that her father should have come across Gormann in the course of a career devoted to public life and foreigners; but bred to regard "niceness" as a normal human trait, the imputations of Nazism were troubling. It was difficult to fit in with Mr Gormann's manner. If lazy and slightly affected, he had not, in their four weeks' acquaintance, shown traces of more sinister faults, still less any tendency towards the enjoyment of human pain. The way Jeremy had sniggered made her wonder. She was innocent of the by-ways of deviation, then returning to fashion, and she did not know if she would recognise a thorough-going sadist if she met one. It was a disconcerting thought, arousing images of the kind crudely fed to the uninitiated by newspapers: riding whips and black underwear came to mind.

Jeremy's snigger rankled. For Evelyn, her brother's sexual

tastes had for some time been in doubt in spite of the eagerness with which her mother attributed him with "girl-friends". She had even allowed herself to speculate on what degree of intimacy had been reached by him and the "guy in the lorry" by the end of their short journey on Friday. But where Jeremy fitted into Mr Gormann's world was the puzzle. If the old man knew her brother, it was odd, to say the least, that he had not mentioned it to her in the course of their frequent conversations over the last few weeks. It suggested that there was something to be kept secret – a vice, perhaps, of the nameless sort which had been passing through her mind, in which he and Jeremy both indulged.

Her relationship with Gormann already seemed strange, difficult enough, without these further exotic touches. She had hoped, in the course of a weekend away from him, to have time to sort things out in her mind, to see, if it were possible, what had happened to her in the last few weeks. Because, undoubtedly, she was different. It now seemed ludicrous for example, that Geoffrey could ever have been so important to her. She was embarrassed to think how much respect she had afforded to his trivial opinions; how often she had turned down opportunities for social life in order to be with him; how much she had been prepared to smother her own increasing distaste for Geoffrey as a lover in order to gratify his feeble little desires. Gormann made her feel exhilarated to have grown out of all this – it lay behind her like childhood. But she felt anxious, to be still in the dark about what kind of a friendship it was that she had contracted.

She did not know where the balance of power, if it was not too grandiose a way of looking at things, lay between them. Clearly, he had much to offer her in the way of physical comfort. He was well-established in London, with a circle of friends and a nice place to live. He was settled; he had so many of the confidences which mere age brings. She felt gauche and juvenile in his presence. She felt that her existence was wispy and fragile, and that her own very limited circle of acquaintances provided her with no strength. She pretended to an air of self-sufficiency in these things. Actually, she was timid and lonely. But, these contrasts helped to explain why she was important to the old man. It was an importance which gave her a power almost equal to his own.

His moods frightened her. She was unable to catch the tone of what he said, although it increasingly seemed to her that he spoke with habitual irony. Some days, he would be excitable, elated, almost dangerously jolly; and, on other occasions, he seemed in the grip of uncontrollable melancholy. But *her* strength lay in the discovery that she slightly, perhaps more than slightly, controlled these changes of temper.

"My body has gone old on me," he had said one evening, in tones of thick, Teutonic self-pity. "But I am still young inside this great hulk. How commonplace it sounds! But I cannot convey to you how odd it feels; and you, my dear, bring it home to me more than anyone!"

"Me?"

"I am back in Heidelburg again when I am with you. I am a young man — vigorous, strong, idealistic. Even handsome. You cannot know what horror it gives me to see these hands: so old and red." He stretched them out, extending his arms so that the cuffs of his shirt slid down beneath his Harris tweed jacket. His cuff-links bore the Papal Arms.

"Would you believe that these hands were white and lean a thousand years ago? Look at them! Look!"

"I like your hands." A lie was the only way to respond. These truthful outbursts of his disturbed her, as they were obviously meant to.

"The knuckles are just lumps!" he protested. "My span is as nothing. I am scarcely able to play the piano any more. I am being devoured by arthritis. You cannot understand —" He had suddenly broken off, seeming cross; whether with himself, or with Evelyn, she could not tell. "Why do I bore you with all this?"

"It doesn't bore me." And then, with the jauntiness her mother so easily assumed in painful moments, she had said, "Everyone gets depressed, you know."

"Ay, madam, 'tis common. But this is more than a depression. I am obsessed. It is a cruelty to inflict it upon you. I have forced my company upon you because I need you. I need," he added hastily, as if to qualify a statement which sounded too strong, "I need the company of the young. I cannot survive without young friends. People of my own age terrify me. I hate being with them. I cannot bear to see their stooping, wrinkled bodies and know that I, too, look like that. It is obscene."

"But your glass is empty," he had added.

They had changed the subject. But his embarrassing observations had merely helped her to articulate what she knew herself to be already doing. She was consciously trying, with a part of herself, to make the old man dependent on her. She wanted to be necessary to his happiness. In part, it seemed an innocent enough wish. "We all like to feel needed," she had thought. But she felt too conscious that she charmed him for it to be wholly safe. She knew that it was unscrupulous, almost wicked; but some of her wanted to use the opportunity for what she could get out of it. Another self threw up its hands at the thought. She was shocking! More, she was deceiving herself.

Friendship with the old, she was beginning to realise, imposed stronger obligations than entanglements with people of her own age. More was at stake. Although she had gone through phases of seeing certain contemporaries every day, there had never been any sense of obligation attached to their meetings. They had happened in the ordinary course of things, because she chanced to like or love the person. But she knew, with frightening certainty, as the train approached Marylebone, that if she were to continue to see Mr Gormann at all, she must choose to be in it up to her neck.

There was time, when she got into London, to go back to her flat, unpack and prepare for supper. She listened to hymns on the wireless while the immersion heater warmed up.

Although assuredly unerotic, she had noticed that since her friendship with Mr Gormann began, she had prepared herself with greater and greater care before meeting him. She had begun regularly to buy the French soap that Geoffrey had once given her for Christmas. Trying to banish an awareness of anything specific from the surface of consciousness, she found that she wanted to be ready for any contingency.

Viewed bluntly, the entanglement with Mr Gormann was problematical precisely because it was impossible to view in sexual terms. As she climbed into her bath, the thought dawned on her, fully articulated, for the first time. If she was to be committed to daily meetings with the old man – more, to recounting to him all her doings and whereabouts when she was not with him – a love affair outside his orbit was going to be impracticable. And, since the days when she had first grown bored with Geoffrey, she had known that she was to a certain extent dependent on sex for her happiness. She felt as if, before she had been sufficiently aware of what was happening, a door had slammed shut behind her. She had been so eager not to go back, that she had not reckoned on how limited the way forward had now become.

Before dressing, she surveyed herself at her dressing-table mirror: really not unbeautiful. She had always particularly liked the line of her stomach, faintly protuberant, but only faintly, before it swooped downwards. Her breasts, too, though slight, were well-formed. They satisfied her. Her shoulders, pale and rounded, framed the whole pleasingly. She felt, looking at herself, some of the anguish which came to one having cooked a rather splendid meal but having no one to eat it.

She was late. "The Day Thou Gavest" had given place to "Brain of Britain". She dressed hurriedly, a black jersey and tights, a red skirt, and made her face up slightly. She had begun to use mascara again – a habit abandoned during a Left-wing phase at Cambridge. Grabbing a handbag, she ran out of the flat and decided that there was no time for a train. She caught a taxi at Prince's Gate.

There was a certain painfulness about the actual moment of seeing Mr Gormann again. She had been thinking about him so

44

much in the last couple of days that it was odd to see him in the flesh, quite apart from the fact that he might have been a friend of Dr Goebbels.

The first awkwardness, unanticipated, was whether to kiss him. They had never been parted for so long before and it seemed, in a way, unnatural not to do so. As they stood facing each other when he opened the door of his apartment, it was clear that the same thought passed through both their minds. There he was – real. That was some comfort, after all these doubts and speculations.

"Dear girl, this gladdens the heart."

She pecked him on the cheek, their first embrace.

"It seems ages."

They giggled.

"Well, come in, come in. I was afraid that you had been run over by a bus, or blown up by a bomb. There are bombs all over London exploding when people least expect them."

Her eye at once darted round the room, by now familiar, for evidence of Mr Gormann's sexual or political proclivities – whips, leather, swastikas. But it was the same, faintly foreign shemozzle: clocks, pipes, an oleograph of the Sacred Heart over the mantelpiece; anti-macassars falling off the backs of chairs; a well-thumbed volume of Schiller lying open on the carpet.

It now seemed even less credible than it had done yesterday evening when her family were discussing him, that this was the same Mr Gormann, mixing Campari and whistling gently.

They clinked glasses, and began small talk. He did not allude to the weekend that had just passed; and, although she felt that she *had* to, if only to establish the ludicrousness of the fears which had arisen so violently, the moment never seemed right. He was on good form, nodding at her benignly and occasionally sipping from his glass. He asked her if she had heard "Any Questions" on the wireless, and regaled her with an account of it. Someone had asked Lord Boothby, Malcolm Muggeridge and the rest how they would occupy themselves in solitary confinement over an extended period.

"All the answers were characteristic." He smiled, behaviour according to type always satisfying him. "A fatuous lady writer whose name I forget claimed she would write a novel. Absurd! Fiction is an essentially social activity. None of them had the presence of mind to give the obvious answer."

"Which is?"

"Why, to commit suicide."

The silence was embarrassing. He had so clearly become serious, though at what point in the conversation it was hard to say.

"Life without people is unthinkable," he added by way of qualification.

"One could always try to escape."

"From solitary confinement? You are so clever, dear girl. You think of everything."

She was always taken in by his flattery. She feasted on it, without noticing at once that his assertion of the impossibility of life without company fastened the bonds between them more tightly.

"We must eat. We must descend into the watery abyss."

In the dispiriting atmosphere of the subterranean restaurant, they had chops, and a bottle of claret, while they looked up at the blue chlorinated waters of the swimming-bath, where men and women darted about like goldfish on the other side of the glass.

In the course of the meal, Evelyn plucked up courage.

"I had a nice weekend."

"A nice little holiday from the old man, eh?"

"Don't be silly."

"Being silly is the prerogative of age."

"You go on too much about being old. You're not *that* old, anyway." She paused. She wondered how old *that* old was, and also whether to raise the subject of her father's or Jeremy's knowledge of Mr Gormann first.

"Pa seems to know quite a lot about you."

"Your father told you how old I am?"

"No. I mean, things about you."

"That sounds very sinister."

"Does it?"

"Well, it would depend on the 'things' perhaps."

"Of course, they weren't sinister things."

"Well, then, what were they?"

"Nothing special. It was just interesting that he had heard of you, I suppose."

"I have heard of him. But that is different. No, no, you are right. You must not protest. Gormann is an out-and-out nonentity. But the English Foreign Office make a practice of busying their heads with nonentities."

"I didn't mean that."

"Ah!" He wiped his mouth gently with his napkin, cheerfully aware of the ease with which he was tying her up in knots.

"It is interesting that you were a theatre critic, for instance," she said, triumphant to have remembered a comparatively innocuous detail from her family's dissection of Mr Gormann's character and history.

"You would not have thought it interesting if you had read my reviews. I have never been able to awaken the slightest interest in anything which I have been paid to do. It is proud of me, perhaps, unbalanced, but there it is. As soon as I undertook that little column, the theatre, hitherto a great source of delight to me, became boring. There have been few jobs that I have been more pleased to give up than that one, but the tendency is a repeated one in my life. I suppose that is why I found life as an academic ultimately uncongenial. I am not, anyway, a natural scholar. But I disliked intensely being paid to read books and say what I thought about them. It was money for jam, I suppose, or money for Homer. But I loathed it. We all know what our friends the psychiatrists have to say about the relationship between money and the activities of the anus."

The word *anus* falling from his lips in the usual precise, pedantic way in which he spoke made Evelyn feel suddenly stiff and uncomfortable. He was winning. She would not press for information if he embarrassed her. But she felt that it would be wrong

47

not to make one more effort to pierce the enigmas made apparent by her weekend at home.

"What was really surprising," she said, after a little silence, "was that Jeremy — my brother — said that he knew you. Knew you personally, I mean . . ."

"And what is surprising about that?" His eyes sparkled.

"Well, nothing, I suppose. Except it's funny we never worked it out before." She laughed uneasily, aware of how unconvincing it must have sounded to be giving him the benefit of the doubt. "I mean, if you know him, and you know me, it is funny, isn't it, that we never put two and two together . . ?"

"What is your brother called?"

"Tradescant. Jeremy Tradescant."

"Is he older or younger than you?"

"Oh, younger. He's still an undergraduate. As you know, of course."

"Is he very close to you?"

She paused before answering.

"In some ways, yes."

"I had a brother. Long dead, of course. He was a year or two older than I was. At a certain stage in our lives, we suddenly stopped being intimate. It's curious how that happens in families. Once more, our friends the psychiatrists probably have an answer for it. A complete parting of the ways. It happened long before I actually left Germany. Then war came, of course, and he was technically on one side, and I on another. The sort of situation of which great tragedy is made; only, in my case, it was impossible to make tragedy of it, since we had absolutely no feelings for each other at all. I was jealous of him, I suppose."

"Didn't you meet after the war?"

"He was dead. Besides, I have never been back to Germany."

"Was he in the army?"

"Not as far as I know. He was a business man. And past the age of military service when war came. He was in the navy in the first one, of course." He sighed heavily. "How *depressing* it is to think

48

of such things."

Anything was preferable to one of Mr Gormann's depressions. Evelyn hastily changed the subject and began to talk about her approaching school term. After coffee, they went upstairs and Mr Gormann played Schubert *Impromptus* on the gramophone.

They sat together on the sofa. She felt glad, really, that she had been unable to pry successfully into his secrets. She was happier not to know.

4

It was nearly May now. The weather was bright, and sun shone through the class-room windows as she taught. She was teaching Trigonometry to the Fifth Form. She ate her lunch with Mrs Todd, the English mistress only a few years older than herself, but, by virtue of parenthood, almost of a different generation. Evelyn listened patiently as her colleague talked of a son's asthma.

After lunch, there was only one lesson and Evelyn had it free. She spent it sitting in the Common Room, copying out names into a markbook in her neat small handwriting.

Evelyn had offered to help coach the girls in tennis this term, and, a little before the end of the last lesson, she went over to the club-house in the square opposite the school to change into her short white skirt and plimsolls. The courts looked golden in the afternoon sun and, for the first day that year, there was real warmth in the sunshine.

Evelyn found a box of new tennis-balls. She took them out on to one of the courts and began to practise serving them over the net. She liked the almost mammal quality of the balls, white and fluffy. And the smell of them always brought back memories to her of her own childhood in Buckinghamshire, when her mother had cut tomato sandwiches for the Amersham Tennis Club. Whenever she smelt tennis-balls, her taste buds supplied tomatoes. And she remembered pleasant afternoons spent teaching Jeremy to play while he was still at his prep-school. He had quickly become better at it than she was.

The girls whom she had arranged to coach came at the time arranged. They wore very expensive little tennis slips. Some of them looked as old as Evelyn did, with developed forms and faces, while some looked as though they were still children. They were all about sixteen.

Evelyn instructed them in the principles of serving a tennis-ball over the net. She told them how to aim the ball so that it fell within the line of the opponent's court. Then each of them served the ball in turn; those of them who did so unsuccessfully were asked to try again. Then she divided them into fours and arranged doubles.

There was one short in the last group to be divided, so Evelyn played with them herself. She enjoyed herself, showing off considerably, with back-hand shots and brilliantly swift footwork. Her actions were so confident and graceful as she moved among her little nymphs that the game might almost have been a dance. When it ended, one of the girls congratulated her on her performance, and she felt pleased.

Then one of them said, "I think your father has come to watch, Miss Tradescant."

Sir Derek was never to be relied upon not to call at the school unexpectedly, now that time hung so heavily on his hands. His arrivals were always rather embarrassing, calling up, quite unfairly, all the feelings of shyness which her parents' visits to Roedean had aroused during her own schooldays. Worse than the shyness itself were the pangs of guilt which accompanied them, since there was no apparent reason to feel ashamed of her parents. It always startled her that many of her contemporaries who had most reason, social or aesthetic, to blush for their families, were often able to cope with the difficulty best, introducing dowdy people with unpleasant accents to their friends without embarrassment. Of course, she was not actually ashamed of her parents, who were both personable, and, in their way, not undistinguished. It was their arrival on alien territory which provoked the awkwardness and the knowledge that her school "self" was not quite the same as her home "self".

"My father? Where?" A sharp nervousness came into her voice as she replied to the girl.

"Over there, Miss Tradescant."

At the other end of the tennis-court, Mr Gormann was looking through the netting at her. Undoubtedly, he looked old enough to be her father, white hair poking out from beneath the brim of a Homburg. But the girl's seemingly innocent mistake was irritating.

"Mind your own business."

"Yes, Miss Tradescant."

"And wipe that complacent smile off your face."

This proved more difficult, but the girl replied "Yes, Miss Tradescant," in the same, faintly wounded tone which suggested that she was suppressing the giggles. Evelyn was not usually snappy with the girls. Embarrassment flustered her. Pimlico Price stood by Mr Gormann, and she was unprepared for him.

"What a pretty sight," he said as she approached them. "I was just telling Theo that it is better than Wimbledon."

"How long were you watching?"

"Only for two or three sets."

"They'll take a bit of knocking into shape."

"They look very nice shapes as they are to me."

He was faintly more handsome than she remembered from the occasion, two years ago at least, when he had come to one of her parties. His face was deeply tanned, and there was the very slightest grey about his temples. Perhaps it was this faint ageing which had improved his appearance. He was tall, and carried himself very upright, throwing back his shoulders a good deal when he talked. When one saw him by the side of Mr Gormann, the old man seemed almost squat, plump certainly. Their faces were quite different, the one angular, broken down the middle with an aquiline nose, and full of rather large, horsey teeth; while the other face would have seemed chubby were it not for the triangle of a white beard adding length to the other features.

"It is yet another aspect of your genius that I barely knew existed, my dear," said Mr Gormann. "John has been trying to explain the rules to me, but without success. The only thing which I have grasped is that when you are losing, you are said to have 'love'."

"It's quite easy." She turned, to see that a group of her pupils were staring at her from the club-house steps. Some of them were whispering and sniggering.

"Excuse me a moment," she said to Mr Gormann.

She walked briskly and officiously up to the girls, and heard herself shouting at them. It sounded shrill and absurd in the presence of other grown-ups. Moreover, it was not how she normally behaved with her pupils. As she walked back to the men, she felt herself blushing. She was struck by the extraordinary look of delight that had passed over Mr Gormann's face. He seemed to have enjoyed the sight of her giving vent to anger – though whether it was the spontaneity of her emotion, or the exposure of her desire to assert her will over the young which had pleased him it was impossible to know.

"I'll just get my things," she muttered quietly, apologetically.

"That's the way," said the old man, alluding to her shouting fit with approval. "A firm hand." In the light of all he had said to her about the education of the young, she had to assume that he was being ironical. The glow of pleasure in his eyes was less easy to account for.

She had not got very far in her reconstructions of the Teutonic past. When Lady Tradescant had asserted that the old man was a friend of Dr Goebbels, Evelyn had made a mental note to the effect that this would change everything. They now met, as normal, without discussing the matter. Acquaintanceship, at least, with Hitler's Minister of Propaganda was not out of the question. Perhaps the whole Nazi leadership, rather than dead or in South America, were discreetly pottering about the carpeted recesses of

Fish Square, paying their rent and giving offence to no one. She would find Mr Gormann no easier to understand had this turned out to be the case. It would have given no more clue to his character than mention of John Price; Richard Evans and "Dodo" de Waal; "poor old" Cedric Tomlinson, and others.

"Please don't bother to change," he said, "I thought that after the strenuous game you have played, you might like to bathe in our pool at Fish Square. We can jump into a taxi at once."

It was an inviting idea. She was wiping sweat from her brow with her wrist as he spoke.

"I ought to tidy up a bit," she said, smiling.

"Please come as you are," said Pimlico Price, a rather inane smile illuminating his face. "You look absolutely ravishing."

She felt like a timid animal, finally encircled by its predators. In the mildest and most civilised way, she was being forced to accompany them to Fish Square. She felt an instinctive distrust of the two men together that she would not have felt of either of them singly. As often in recent weeks, she was overtaken by a vague impression of fear, born of a suspicion which no outward evidence could fully justify, that the whole of her friendship with Mr Gormann, which had seemed to her so delightfully spontaneous and impulsive, had actually been deliberated by the old gentleman himself. Her wiser self told her that this was wild paranoia. How, after all, could he have known that he would meet her in Kensington Gardens, still less persuade her, a total stranger, to give him tea in an expensive hotel? It must have all been the purest chance. But it was beginning to acquire the air of a conspiracy.

As she returned to the club-house to collect her things, leaving the two men waiting for her near the tennis-courts, she wondered why it was that people had told her so little. By accident, it appeared, she had walked into a circle that already knew about her. She had encountered an old man known to her father and to her brother. And that old man, in turn, had friends who knew her independently, through Geoffrey. Everything linked up. But no one had thought to tell her very much.

"Damn it," she thought, as she put her racket back in its press, "I haven't even asked them. They probably think it very queer of me to have taken it all so much for granted."

She delegated the responsibility of locking up the club-house to one of the senior girls, gathered up her clothes in a canvas bag and strolled back towards Mr Gormann and Pimlico Price. She could not help feeling that they looked solid, amiable sort of fellows.

"Excellent, my dear," said Mr Gormann, "Excellent. Now, John, if you would be so kind as to find us some transport."

"It might almost be quicker to walk down to the Brompton Road," Evelyn said. "It is only two minutes away, and there are thousands of taxis driving up and down there at this time of day."

They decided to act upon this counsel, and, after two or three minutes' stroll through blossomy crescents and squares, they found themselves emerging into the busy thoroughfare somewhere between Harrods and the Oratory.

They found a taxi with no difficulty. It took them a long time to reach Fish Square because of the evening traffic, but it was such a pleasant drive through Sloane Square and Chelsea that none of them much minded the delays.

It was a love of London, perhaps, which was the most noticeable thing that Evelyn and Mr Gormann had in common. Geoffrey had appeared to regard the metropolis as a glorious playground; and that had been fun. They had tramped about in search of its grotesquer features, social and architectural. She had laughed, in the best of times because she was happy, not because she could see the joke. She really found Mr Gormann's love of London more agreeable. It was faintly sentimental. He was horrified by the changes, and there were a good many areas, Holborn and Bloomsbury, for example, where he refused to go on the grounds that they had been "vandalised".

He belonged to all kinds of organisations to save London, SWAG being the most bizarre and the most recent of his enthusiasms, the Save Willesden Action Group.

"John says that I can never resist a lost cause," was one of the things he often said when telling her about campaigns to save a terrace, a church or a square from demolition. It was all of a piece with his terror of old age, a desire to arrest or reverse the ravages of time. "People look older and London looks newer as time passes; and I don't know which depresses me more." But, in a strange way, it seemed to give him a kind of painful satisfaction that London was being spoilt. The modern world was behaving "in character". As façades changed, and buildings vanished, he liked to speak of them as if he alone possessed the secret of what they had been like before. To hear him speak, one would have thought that nobody but he could remember the neo-classical arch at Euston Station.

"You should have come here twenty years ago," he would say, staring at a pile of new office-blocks. "There was the loveliest of Victorian warehouses – a real masterpiece." The more incredulous the response, the greater the feeling of superiority that it evidently gave him.

Evelyn did not exactly love architecture. But she loved knowing where she was, and London was a good place for testing one's sense of direction. In this way, Mr Gormann's London talk complemented her own.

She sat between the two men in the back of the taxi, and gave a little commentary on the places they were passing. "Lower Sloane Street . . . So we will be going over Ebury Bridge." Mr Gormann meanwhile looked out of another window and let out gentle moans of disappointment at the sight of neon shop fronts or houses painted in ill-chosen colours.

Pimlico Price did not say much, but he appeared to be happy. Having been accustomed to have an establishment in London all his life, he was incapable of approaching it with the zest of strangers like Mr Gormann and Evelyn. He knew London pretty well, and could probably find his way about just about anywhere in town, provided he was in a taxi.

Whenever the taxi swayed, Evelyn was thrown, gently but firmly against one man or the other. Even by sitting quite straight

56

and with her legs tightly together, her bare calves still found themselves brushed occasionally by a trouser.

In Chichester Street, with Fish Square in view, they queued for a long time at the traffic lights.

"Heard anything of Geoffrey?" Pimlico asked her. It was said in a kindly tone of voice which implied an understanding of what had happened between them.

"No, no I haven't."

"He's left Princeton. Yes, already. Robert Matheson – do you know Robert? No. Well, Robert heard from him the other week. It was not made very clear what was happening on that front."

"He fell in love, you know," she said.

She said it as if he had contracted some rather shameful disease.

Pimlico laid his hand on her arm, as if to comfort her. It was kind of him, but entirely unnecessary. She felt no regrets about not seeing Geoffrey any more. As the taxi put them down at Fish Square, she rather hoped they would drop the subject.

They entered by way of the "Sports Club and Restaurant", rather than going into Kempenfelt House. The old man said that he was going to sit in the bar while the young people swam.

The bar overlooked the swimming-pool. Many people actually took drinks to the water's edge. Mr Gormann settled himself in a kind of gallery above the pool and sipped Campari soda.

Pimlico showed Evelyn where she should change, and then sauntered off to "get into his togs", as he termed it.

"I must remember to have a wee-wee," he remarked. "Swimming always makes me want to go."

It was only when she was alone in her changing cubicle that she remembered that she had not brought a swimsuit. The game of tennis, followed by half an hour in a taxi, made her long for the cold water eagerly. Besides, she would be made to look highly ridiculous to have come all this way for the purpose of swimming, unless she swam.

She rummaged through the canvas bag a second time. Sometimes she kept a spare swimsuit with her other games things; but there was none to be seen.

She stood up, naked, and surveyed herself in the looking glass, wondering what would happen if she were to appear for a bathe like that. The idea was vaguely appealing. And she was conscious, as she ran her fingers over her white skin and half turned to see her back in the glass, that such an exposure would have an appropriateness on the present occasion.

She opened the cubicle door. There was no one else about. Outside, there were showers, and other cubicles with young ladies' belongings in them. There were also hooks, where several swimsuits were hanging up.

She walked over to the hooks and selected a black one. The owner would surely not mind. She held the garment against herself. It was faintly too short, and rather too big about the bust. But she could just about fit into it. It was very slightly damp.

She went back into her cubicle and put it on. It was of a very simple design, the sort which she had seen her father wearing in old photographs taken before the war, plain black, with straps over the shoulder.

Borrowing a towel from a different hook, she strode out.

Pimlico Price was waiting for her at the edge of the pool, sporting swimming drawers of a bright yellow. He had a young-looking, rather bony body, but there were thick grey hairs on his chest. Evelyn thought how odd people looked without their clothes. You wouldn't have expected Pimlico to be quite so hairy; and not grey hairs . . .

Mr Gormann was standing up and leaning over the chromium bar in the gallery at the other end of the pool. He waved, a cigarette in hand, and they waved back.

Evelyn was first in the water. When she bobbed to the surface again, her bright red hair became instantly black, clinging to the sides of her head like seaweed. First she did about twenty strokes of crawl with her face down in the water. The chlorine from the pool began to sting her eyes and she lolled over to do a leisurely back-stroke. Pimlico Price did the breast-stroke in the deep end, with quick, nervous movements of the arms. He bounced up in the water and smiled at her when their eyes met.

Dytiscus marginalis, Evelyn remembered. It may unexpectedly turn up in any pond of water, but is chiefly to be met with in a pond with plenty of weeds in it.

"I'll race you!" she called out enthusiastically.

"I'm not very fast," he laughed back.

They swam to the edge of the deep end and held on to the tiling breathlessly. His appearance, too, now that he was completely wet and shivering, had changed completely. His chest had become dark and bedraggled.

"Two lengths of breast-stroke. That's what you seem to be best at," she said firmly.

"On your marks, get set, go!"

From his chromium bar, where he drank a second glass of Campari soda, Mr Gormann watched tenderly as the young glistening forms sported in the water below him.

Evelyn won the race easily. Then she splashed Pimlico with water and swam out of his reach. Helpless and panting, he protested and set off in pursuit of her, gasping for breath and splashing a good many people apart from Evelyn in the process. Soon, he was exhausted, and swam to the edge of the pool. He tried to climb out but Evelyn pulled him back in again with a huge splash.

"Oh! Oh! I say!"

He went under water, and by the time he had surfaced, spluttering like a sea-lion, she was standing on the edge laughing. She was too much for him. He came out of the steps at the shallow end, shaking like an old spaniel.

She was drying herself with a towel when he came up to her.

"Let's have one more race," she suggested.

"I think Theo is trying to tell us something," he said.

"Don't make excuses. I won!" She was exultant. She had forgotten about Mr Gormann.

"He looks a bit worried. We had better go and see what he wants. He seems to have picked up a friend with big titties."

When he had rubbed his hair, he began to look almost as he had done when they first arrived. They walked up the iron steps to the gallery to Mr Gormann, who did, indeed, look anxious.

"It is really most unfortunate," he said, "but there is a lady here, my dear, who believes you to have taken her swimsuit."

"And my towel. If that isn't my towel she's holding."

A middle-aged lady in a flowery summer frock pointed at Evelyn with helpless gestures of outrage. Her cheeks were flushed and pink, and her appearance was made faintly extraordinary by the fact that she was wearing a blue rubber bathing-cap on her head, and blue rubber flippers on her feet. It looked rather as if, should one peel off the silky layers of her outer clothing, more expanses of blue rubber would be revealed.

"Are you accusing my friend of being a thief?" asked Pimlico with surprising bluntness.

"It's not fair, that's all I say," said the blue rubber lady.

"What makes you say that bathing-costume is yours?" Pimlico continued aggressively. "It's like hundreds of other bathing-costumes."

"I mended the strap with green cotton myself," said the lady. "I always recognise it by that."

"I bought it in Selfridges," said Evelyn.

Once back in her cubicle, she rapidly peeled off the swimsuit, wrung it out and hung it up on the hook where it had been before. Then she changed into her black velvet trousers and put on a lambswool jersey.

"Sorry to be so long," she said when she rejoined the others. "I dried my hair on one of those machines."

"Outrageous person," Pimlico said. His hair was still wet, combed back and clinging tightly to his head. It made him look like a teddy boy.

"I'm sorry to be a bit rude to her," he added. "But people just don't go round stealing bathing costumes. If you ask me, she was a bit bonkers."

Mr Gormann had bought drinks for them all and smiled inscrutably while Pimlico delivered himself of these opinions. It was impossible to tell whether he had seen through her lie to the blue rubber lady; or what he thought of the incident. Evelyn hoped the evening could pass with no more allusion to it.

"You behaved as one would have expected, my dear. My dears. *Santé*."

"Absolutely bonkers," Pimlico added, as if, after a moment's reflection on his choice of adverb, it had seemed too mild.

The conversation did change. As Mr Gormann spoke, always fluently, and with little gestures of the hands, Evelyn again tried to imagine him as her parents had described: an international undesirable; if not actually a National Socialist, at least a friend of the more diabolical members of the movement. The subsequent pretence of pacifism, to which Sir Derek had alluded, was presumably still kept up, so that any traces of his former self would be hard to discern . . .

But it all seemed too fantastic. Sir Derek and Lady Tradescant must have been mistaken. Evelyn had never met any friends of Dr Goebbels before, so she had no criterion by which to decide what they might be like. But she felt unwilling to regard Mr Gormann as evil. She felt unwilling, if it came to that, to regard any of her friends as evil. Of course, there were murderers and tyrants about, but she had never encountered one, and, in all senses that mattered, they did not belong to the realms of real life. Her acquaintance with nasty people was extensive – gossips, moaners, liars. But Mr Gormann was not even a nasty person.

Nevertheless, the judgments that her parents had made of the old man's character lent him an unpleasant aura which she longed to dispel. It could only be done by questions.

There had been another explosion in London that day. A restaurant, full of what the newspapers called clients and lunchers, had been blown up in Chelsea. The old man was distressed by it, and he seemed still more distressed by Pimlico's tasteless jokes.

"Waiter, there's a bomb in my soup."

61

"Talking of bombs, I gather you were once very interested in Ban the Bomb," Evelyn heard herself saying.

"CND and all that? No, I can't say I was. Theo is more the man to ask."

"Perhaps Evelyn meant to address me?" If there was a hint of rebuke in Mr Gormann's voice, Pimlico did not notice it.

"And in what way," he added, after a long pause, "do people gather information about an unknown quantity like Gormann?"

"Pa said you had been a pacifist. My father. Last time I went home, it must have been."

The introduction of an air of vagueness, intended to suggest nonchalance, actually gave the impression that she had discussed Mr Gormann so often with her family that she found it difficult to keep separate conversations apart in her mind. But the old man betrayed no signs of alarm. He merely shook his head as if he were going to say nothing. And then he spoke.

"I happened to believe that it was dangerous to contemplate the elimination of the entire human race. That was an idea which was considered unreasonable by the British Government of the day. And by the British Foreign Office, presumably, although the policies of those two bodies do not always coincide. That was why I marched to Aldermaston."

"Evelyn's too young to remember it all," said Pimlico. "How old that makes one feel. Beatniks, duffle coats and all that."

"It was a point of principle," said Mr Gormann quietly.

How totally opaque and impenetrable he was! Evelyn had learnt to live with her father's impenetrability; it seemed normal by now. But Sir Derek was remote by very obvious techniques of moderation and conversational discretion. His bland smile would crease his waxy cheeks, and his eyes would suddenly become as dead as marbles behind his spectacles if you asked him a question which was out of order. The only questions which really fell into this category were ones to which Sir Derek knew no answer. And it was the frequency of his failures to reply, the solid and widespread nature of his ignorances, which lent an impression of absolute discretion to his manner. Mr Gormann, she felt, concealed the answers to questions for altogether different reasons. But she felt no less cut off from him than she had done, all her life, from her father. Somehow, she had hoped from their initial encounter in Kensington Gardens that this was not to be so and that their friendship would flower into revelation and knowledge of each other. But the old man's little speech about the Bomb, although it sounded drearily sincere, blew like a cold wind into her heart.

Pimlico Price continued the conversation about duffle coats. He spoke as if the late fifties were so long ago that there was something remarkable about being able to remember them at all.

"Another part of the equipment," he dilated in a leisurely voice, "of the protest marcher of those misty times, was the 'sloppy joe', a large woollen jersey, polo-necked if you were a man and V-necked, worn back to front if you were a lady. It used to show off the titties rather nicely, wool. Remember the stuff? Came off sheep, I believe. 'There is no substitute for wool.' That takes you back."

He was slightly drunk. As his hair dried out, Evelyn saw his appearance fit into the image she had remembered of him since his appearance at her party. She was amused by his plummy flow of talk, but also mildly cross with him for having taken Mr Gormann away from the subject of his early life. "Pimlico is a great talker," someone had said to her ages ago in Cambridge. There certainly seemed to be modesty in Mr Gormann's claims that he himself was the most boring man in London. But she liked the way that thick hairs protruded like a grey hearth-rug from the top of Pimlico's open-necked shirt.

"We are keeping Evelyn too long," said Mr Gormann at the first pause in Pimlico's talk. "And, indeed, we have kept her far too long already. John, go and ring up for a taxi."

It had not occurred to her that she would not be dining with them. She felt embarrassingly gauche and young. It was like being an undergraduate again, realising that one had outstayed one's welcome, but not having the social equipment which would enable one to depart gracefully. She had done it constantly in her first year at the university: found herself being almost pushed out of houses at seven o'clock to which she had been invited for tea. Nervousness made her do it then. Once someone had told her, "When they offer you a glass of sherry, it means they want you to bugger off," she was all right. Now, once more, she felt all the awkwardness of being in the presence of people more grown-up than herself, and not knowing how to behave. She hoped they did not recognise how put out she felt. Of course, she could hardly have expected to be asked to dinner. But she silently cursed herself for having needled Mr Gormann about the CND. And, now, for standing there like a fool, blushing deeply to the roots of her carrotty hair.

They all stood up. She suddenly felt, in the way that shyness provokes irrational opinions, that they had only invited her there to torture her. Mr Gormann *did* seem cruel, after all. She tried to fight the impression, but it would not go away.

"Let me take your bag," said Pimlico generously. She made a mental note that she must call him "John" before she left.

"I will make my adieux here, my dear," said Mr Gormann. He was as genial as always. There was nothing in his bearing to suggest crossness.

"I will be in touch," said Evelyn.

"I shall be extremely cross with you if you are not. Come and bathe again soon, perhaps?" He waved his cigarette case and sat down at his table again almost as soon as she and Pimlico had turned away. It was the first time she had ever parted from the old gentleman without feeling the palm of his hand linger momentarily on her bottom.

"Theo is extremely fond of you," said Pimlico Price in serious tones, as soon as their feet touched the carpeted corridors once more. "His life has been quite transformed since he met you. I only hope . . . God, this sounds awfully sententious of me. I just hope he won't be too much hurt by it all, that's all."

"Thank you," she said blearily. She had not the faintest notion of what he was talking about. "I like Mr Gormann enormously too."

"Everyone's frightfully amused by your calling him 'Mr Gormann', of course." He had resumed his plummy facetious tones. "I shouldn't be surprised if it starts to catch on as the latest 'in' joke."

"Everyone?"

"I shouldn't think anyone has called him Mr Gormann since he left Germany. Everyone calls him Theo."

"Oh. I should like to know more about his past," she added frankly.

"You and I must get together. Theo doesn't awfully like being cross-questioned as you've perhaps gathered. There have been people who have made life fairly hard for him because he was born of an old German family. And his brother, of course, *was* involved with Havenstein at the time when the Mark collapsed."

"Was Havenstein a Nazi?"

"Heavens, no. That was in 1923."

"I don't know about things like that."

"But Karl Gormann *did* for a time support the Nazis, to extricate himself from the disgrace of having been party to the financial ruin of his country. You can imagine how awful it was for Theo."

"Yes."

"Theo never really identified himself with Germany, you know. His mother was half Welsh. He very nearly took her surname once."

"What was it?"

"Schlick. Her father was Czechoslovakian, but they lived in Aberystwyth."

"So it wouldn't have made much difference."

"I suppose not."

"Thank you for telling me all this."

They hovered by the large reception desk, while she tried to bring herself to use his Christian name.

"It would almost be quicker to go out and hail a taxi myself," she said.

"I'll come with you."

"It's been nice to knit old friendship up," said Pimlico.

Evelyn was being held in his arms and kissed. It was a very clumsy, slobbery sort of kiss. She smelt a mixture of sweat, chlorine and after-shave lotion.

She sat in the back of the taxi waving as Pimlico Price's amiable face shrank to a dot in the distance.

5

It was Saturday morning. Evelyn went shopping for food in Old Brompton Road. Jeremy had announced that he was coming to stay in her flat for the weekend.

Sun shone brightly on the street, and the mildest of breezes blew. Evelyn felt exhilarated by not having to teach. She wore, ostentatiously, a cheese-cloth blouse and blue denim trousers, garments unthinkable for the class-room.

It had been rather a full week. She had only seen Mr Gormann twice since she had been to bathe at Fish Square, although he had rung her up every day.

Pimlico Price's somewhat sententious advice to her created a mild feeling of awkwardness now whenever she met Mr Gormann or heard his voice. She had been shielding herself from the knowledge that she was important to him and trying to convince herself that it was perfectly normal for an elderly gentleman to seek almost daily contact with a woman a third of his age. It was difficult enough to find that she was growing to love Mr Gormann, if love was the right word for the mild restlessness which disturbed her on the days when they did not meet. But to contemplate his loving her was intolerable. It made it all too serious.

She wondered, too, what part Pimlico Price played in all this drama. There had been something calculated and stagey about the way it had been arranged that they should meet. Since, after all, she was mildly acquainted with him already, it was strange that it had to be Mr Gormann who reintroduced them, and Mr Gormann who brought their meeting to an end. Were they now supposed to meet independently? Was the old man consciously trying to push them together? It was impossible to say.

Pimlico had rung her up the morning after their swim together to ask if she would come to the opera with him on Saturday.

"They're doing *Così* at Covent Garden," he had said, and although she did not begin to understand what he meant, she had accepted eagerly. Jeremy had rung almost at once to say he was coming to town, and she had rung Pimlico back to ask if her brother could be of the party. Rather surprisingly, he had said that it would be better if they arranged to meet another time. He withdrew his invitation to the opera. It was not what she had intended to happen at all. Of course, if it had been difficult to get another ticket at short notice, Jeremy could just have supped with them afterwards.

"I'm not very good at parties *à trois*," Pimlico said. "You see your brother and I'll ring you up some time next week. All right? 'Bye now."

It had not been all right. It was odd. He had sounded hurt. But he had no right to be. He was not Evelyn's lover. And even if he had been, there was no reason why he should have refused to meet Jeremy.

She bought a large cabbage at the greengrocers; two lettuces; a cucumber, and half a pound of tomatoes. They were still a fearful price. She had no clear plans about what to do with them all, but she decided that if she bought some cold viands at the Delicatessen, and a little cheese, it would probably help them to get through the weekend and avoid starvation.

Slightly tired, she sat down at a table on the street corner outside an Italian restaurant. She would have some coffee and read her post, which she had slipped into her shoulder bag on her way out of her flat without opening. Since one letter was from America and one from her bank, she had no desire to read either.

She looked first at a postcard reproduction of Piero della Francesca's *Baptism of Christ* which Jeremy had sent from Oxford. She was transported for a moment by even so faint an echo of the great painting, her favourite in the National Gallery, and one of the few works of art which moved her. She was enchanted by the impassivity of the faces, and by the way the central figure seemed to have no weight, but simply to hover in the centre of the picture. In the background, an eager neophyte was getting his head stuck in a shirt as he pulled it over his head in preparation for naked immersion. On the back of the card was written, *See you demain, dearest Sis, as arranged. Will bring booze! L. o. l. J.*

She opened the letter from the bank next. It was merely a computerised statement of her current account informing her that she had £63.58p to her credit. There were no major bills coming up, and she was to be paid again in a few days time; so there was nothing to be distinctly worried about. She was depressed by the fact, though, that she could never really *do* anything with the sort of money that she earned. A good holiday would ruin her for two or three months.

The letter from America was not in the least welcome to her. It was typed, and from New York. The name and address of the sender had not been filled in in the space provided, but she knew that it was from Geoffrey.

My dear, dear Evelyn
Life in this benighted colony is really less fun than one might have hoped. But that's partly because I've broken my leg and have been recovering in New York. Thank God for Insurance Companies. The bill for setting a leg over here is colossal.

Do you remember old Maxwell-Jacobs? He was in chambers with Nicholas. He turned up here the other day, rather improbably. Otherwise, company is limited to Americans, of whom there appear to be an inordinate number on this side of the

Atlantic.

I find that I missed you rather more than I had feared. I think it was a mistake for us to split up after all the good times . . . They say that teaching pays well over here.

Ever, G.

She read it once, and then stuffed it into her bag again. It simply embarrassed her. No other feeling was noticeable. She wished that she had not read it. It made her feel that people were staring at her and she did not know where to look.

Not two months had passed since she had assumed herself to be romantically attached to Geoffrey. Now, a letter from him seemed to be referring to two selves that no longer had any existence. She had changed almost absolutely, she felt, since the end of the affair. But Geoffrey, it seemed, had not. He was still as egocentric as before, expecting one to take an interest in trivialities like a broken leg. They were not terms on which she wanted to know anyone again.

And yet, how strange it was that she really had *known* Geoffrey. It was unthinkable that she could ever know Mr Gormann so well. For one thing, he was so much, much older; and whole areas of the past remained unmentioned in their talk, not because he was necessarily suppressing anything, but because he could not possibly remember it all. Geoffrey's life had been almost as short as her own. He was twenty-seven, and could remember everything that had happened to him since he was three. On reflection, she thought, it had not been much. He had been to two prep-schools; to Radley, to Trinity Hall; and then Lincoln's Inn. Now this American nonsense. It was very much the sort of life on which one could keep tabs.

Now, she felt hugely, immeasurably bored by it. She had heard his imitations of the schoolmasters and dons who had happened to cross his path. She had heard all about his parents, and met them twice. She had been to a party of his sister's, who was a rather bossy lady, two years his senior married to a Chartered Accountant in Hove . . . She had known it all already, known it all. The fact was, she could live without him perfectly satisfactorily, and his letter was nothing but an irritant.

She remembered a comment she had once read on *Scolytidae* in *British Beetles, their homes and habits*: "A great deal has been learned respecting the life history of these, because it has been so easily followed." Were her dreams ever to be fulfilled, and were she ever to become a full-time coleopterist, she would look for rarer sport.

One of the great advantages of not having Geoffrey in her life any more was that it enabled her to get along so much better with Jeremy. The boy had always been jealous of her lover. She knew it, though nothing had been said. She was determined that this weekend should draw them closer together; and, if possible, reveal more to her about Jeremy's knowledge of Mr Gormann.

This was so odd, Jeremy's knowing Mr Gormann, that she found it almost incredible. She kept telling herself that she had misheard, when the boy had referred to him as "Theo". But there was clearly no getting it out of Mr Gormann himself until he was ready to impart the information. It must all be allowed to emerge, was what she told herself. She would simply observe, and events would begin to unfold themselves.

When she had finished her coffee, she went back to the flat and awaited Jeremy's arrival. His train was due in Paddington at twelve o'clock, so she was expecting him for lunch.

He arrived at about two, explaining that he had decided to hitch-hike from Oxford, and it had taken him longer than he had expected. He was wearing a pale blue jersey and black corduroy trousers; and baseball boots on his feet. Evelyn was disconcerted to see that he was growing a moustache.

"It suits you," she said, kissing him.

"Am I late? It took me hours to get a lift."

"Donkey. Why didn't you get the train?"

"I felt like hitching."

"Hard up?" She opened a tin of tomato soup as she spoke, hoping that she gave the appearance of domestic competence and motherliness.

71

"A bit. I say, you wouldn't have a cigarette by any chance?"

"There are some in the drawer over there. No the other one."

"Rotten old English ones."

"You can have them if you like."

He lit up. "Have you given up then?"

"No. I've hardly ever started. Now, there's soup on the boil. And then garlic sausage and ham. The meal will be the same this evening, and tomorrow at lunch time. It's simpler."

"Undeniably."

"Clever dick."

"So, how are you, sis?" He came over and held her tightly from behind, his head resting on her shoulders.

"Not so bad. Term is being rather boring, but one gets paid for it. I hate my Fourth Form, but otherwise the children are un-noticeable."

"Quite."

"What are you going to do when you've finished lazing round the flesh-pots of Oxford?"

"This is the problem." He released hold on her, or rather, she struggled free to lay the table, and he carried on smoking. "Any ideas?"

"I thought that you were all set to become a publisher?"

"Harder than it sounds. I don't suppose that I want to do any-thing, really. Anything that makes money is so boring – and if jobs don't make pots of money, what's the point of doing them."

"It's demoralising not to work," she said seriously, talking to herself.

"I would happily be demoralised if I could afford it."

"Now, we can eat."

They ate the soup with Hovis and then tucked into the salad. Jeremy ate ravenously and silently.

"Pa wants you to go into the Foreign Office. There could be worse things, I suppose."

"Such as?"

"I don't know."

"Quite."

They ate for a while in silence.

"Pimlico Price has offered to help me to get into the City, but I'm not sure I want to be a big financier either."

"Who is Pimlico Price?" she asked, putting on as blank an expression as was possible in the circumstances.

"Your new boy-friend, I gather." The corners of his mouth turned up mischievously as he spoke.

"I haven't got a boy-friend," she said.

"Of course not."

"Anyway, why does everyone call him 'Pimlico' Price. And he isn't my boy-friend. I've only met him about twice. Really, Jeremy, you are a donkey."

"I gather that you went bathing together and that he defended you from the assaults of jealous women at the swimming-pool."

"One silly woman, who was cross because I was wearing her bathing clothes."

"Understandably."

"How do you know all these characters, anyway?"

"All?"

"Mr Gormann, Pimlico Price. You probably know Richard Evans and David, for all I know; or whoever they are."

"I could hardly avoid knowing Dodo de Waal. He was at school with me and then at the same college in Oxford for a year."

"Come clean, Jeremy. I want to know."

"I was wondering when you were going to ask."

"So was I."

"OK. Now, where do I begin? You see, once you know one of that crowd, you know them all. I've told you about Dodo, which is how I met Richard. And I met Pimlico at an OE dinner, believe it or not."

"Pimlico?"

"Yes."

"But I still don't see how you seem to know them all so . . . I don't know quite how to put this, but it seems like a conspiracy to

73

me. I mean, why don't Pimlico and Mr Gormann admit that they know you?"

"Perhaps you haven't asked them. I hardly know Theo, actually. I've only ever met him at Pimlico's place. But, I say, sis, while we're on this gruesome subject, it wasn't the most tactful thing in the world letting Theo ring you up at home. Pa would go through the roof if he thought I'd really been moving in that world."

"What world?"

"Now you're being coy."

There was a long pause during which Evelyn thought she might very well be about to be sick.

"I'll have a cigarette after all," she said.

Jeremy's expression was one of that blank smiling helplessness which only adorns the faces of animals or the very young when they have done something wrong, but do not know quite what it is. Shit on the carpet.

"I thought you knew," he said.

"No. No I didn't." She sounded like a school-ma'am. "Oh, Jeremy, forgive me for being so obtuse."

She stood up, and he stood up and they squeezed each other in a long hug.

"Come and sit down. We'll do the washing-up later." She led him to the sofa in an elder-sisterly manner, holding his hand as she spoke.

"You may very well . . . Well, I don't want to be matronly, but you may very well *change*. You're rather young."

He kissed her on the forehead.

"Absurd and lovable sister. Of course I shall change. Everyone does. But I may still go on being naughty. Naughty in that way, I mean."

"And . . . are you . . . naughty with Pimlico?"

"Sometimes. Are you?"

"What do you think I am?" She looked gloriously red-haired and defiant.

"A nut-case. But beloved of every queen in London. Every

queen who matters, that is."

"You don't mean to tell me that Mr Gormann is . . ."

"Roughly speaking. You would not have guessed?"

"Not in a million years. You see . . ." She blew out smoke in a long sigh. There was a sort of relief about knowing. "You see, I'm not really very much aware of that side of life."

"I thought you told me once you had a crush on a girl at school. What was her name? Julia something."

"That's different somehow."

"Is it?"

"Yes. School is always different."

"You ought to know. You were eager enough to get back there and surround yourself with girls."

He was hurting her. School *had* been different, though. Julia had been nothing to her. She was surprised that she had bothered to tell Jeremy about her. But she had never told him about Miss Uxley, the Maths mistress.

They called it having a "crack" on somebody at her school. A "crush" was something you had on girls younger than yourself. Hot, painful, agonised fantasies had haunted her, with Miss Uxley at the centre of them. She would blush if Miss Uxley spoke to her. Once, when giving her back a piece of work in class, this woman's hand had met Evelyn's. It was a memorable moment. She had been convinced that Miss Uxley had allowed their knuckles to touch each other for longer than had been strictly necessary. As she stared up tremulously into the great dark eyes of her beloved, she had discerned the barest flicker of emotion. The moment had passed.

She sprang up. "Let's *do* something, for heaven's sake. We could go to the V and A, for instance."

"OK."

"You don't sound very enthusiastic."

"Evie, you won't tell Ma and Pa, will you? You see they wouldn't understand at all."

"I won't tell them. But they are bound to find out."

"If they find out, they find out. I just don't want you to tell

75

them, that's all. Besides, as you say, I might 'change' — whatever that is."

"I promise not to tell them on one condition."

"What's that?"

"That you let me shave off that silly moustache."

"But you said you liked it."

"Do you accept my conditions?"

"I'm not sure I do."

"Very well, then. I shall tell."

They were five and nine years old again.

"If you must. My razor is in my bag. I'll get it."

He returned, blushing, and holding out a sponge-bag.

"It's too bad."

"Perhaps."

"'This hurts you more than it hurts me,' I suppose."

"Precisely."

She was rolling up her sleeves. "Now what's this?" She picked up his funnel of shaving-cream. "Looks like a thing of fly-spray." She squeezed it hard, causing a little snow-storm to cover his lap.

"Steady on."

"Sorry. Didn't know it would come out so fast."

She picked up a little of the foam from his fingers and gently pasted it on to his upper lip.

"Now, where's your razor?"

"In there. This is mere sadism."

She brandished the little safety-razor melodramatically and bared her teeth, letting out a low growl.

"Whatever happened to that girl-friend of yours that Ma is always talking about?" she asked, as she began to shave him. The skin on his face was extraordinarily soft.

"Which one, dear, I have so many?"

"I met her once in your rooms."

"Jennifer? She is all right, as far as I can tell. Why do you ask?"

"What does she think of your goings on?"

"How do you mean?"

"Jeremy, do keep still or I'll cut your throat."

The moustache was gone. Little smudges of cream remained around the edges of his nostrils.

"I don't know what you're asking," he said. "Are you saying, 'When did I last fuck my girl-friend?' or 'Does she know that I'm gay?' or what? And why the hell should I tell you? You tell me nothing about your private life."

"Sorry. I can't help being curious."

"You're as bad as Ma."

"Ma knows everything without having to ask. She must be telepathic."

"So that's what telepathic means."

"What?"

"Reading other people's letters. Listening in to telephone calls."

"She doesn't. Anyway, how do you know?"

"I'm telepathic myself."

"Look, what are we going to do this afternoon? It's nearly a quarter to four already."

"I am like Samson shorn of his strength. I am much too weak to do anything."

They decided to visit the Victoria and Albert Museum, which was just round the corner from Evelyn's flat. Jeremy liked the rooms full of English China and Pottery; and although tier upon tier of plates and tea-pots and vases in glass cases bored Evelyn to distraction, distraction was what she felt most need of at that moment. It was quite restful having Jeremy as a companion. He took such an intense interest in the exhibits that one was not obliged to make much conversation.

Evelyn remembered Mr Gormann saying that all museums, whatever they were exhibiting, conspired to make us believe in evolution. There was something about the arrangement of the English pottery which made one sense this. Nobody, standing in front of a case of early Rockingham bowls and candlesticks, could fail to think them more exquisite and clever and refined than the heavy brown slipware which characterised the late mediaeval exhibits. And yet, somewhere about 1820, the thing appeared to have gone too far. The fruits and flowers and figurines of High Victorian Worcester or Chelsea ware seemed repugnantly full of shape and colour, so that one longed for the brown artlessness at the beginning of the series. One could only see the truth of Evolution when Human Nature was just past its best. Once it had been pointed out that we are all descended from the apes, we became hungry for the simplicity of the savage life.

At the moment, Evelyn was reading Darwin's treatise on the Earth Worm, and had decided that his was the greatest of genius.

This deviation of Jeremy's was a piece of High Victorian frippery; an example, surely, of Human Nature past its best. But more, of course, it affected her own life most radically. Her first thought, when the truth of the matter dawned was that this would change everything. But she now wondered what she had meant by "this" and "change" and "everything".

She had remarkably little knowledge of the "mating" habits of the "world" of which Jeremy had declared himself to be a casual member. She tried to visualise what they *did* and found it impossible. Men's bodies are so appallingly badly designed. What mattered more than what they did was who "they" were. If "they" were Jeremy and Pimlico, this was truly disturbing.

It was hard to fit into her picture of the man: the legendary Pimlico – "That's a nice pair of titties." Gossip can frequently be inaccurate – perhaps its saving virtue is that it nearly always is. But Evelyn felt surprised that it could be as wrong as all this. She remembered stories of his coming up to Cambridge on the "dolly" train on Friday evenings, undergraduate parties at which he chatted up girls . . . Geoffrey's accounts of him had always accepted, elaborated the received opinion. And now she had her own more recent experiences to fit into the picture: the faintly crude, apparently heterosexual bawdy, the kiss as she got into her taxi.

She had always assumed, since she had begun to think about Pimlico Price, that he led an honourable, though dull way of life; in the City for most of the year, and dashing back to his "place" in

Scotland as often as possible. Her mind supplied salmon rivers, lochs, mountains losing themselves in the clouds; bracken alive with beetles.

This man – was he forty-five? – sometimes went to bed with her brother. She wondered, with half of herself, why this statement should seem more striking than an observation that he sometimes played chess with Jeremy, or that they belonged to the same club. But the other half of her mind recoiled; not with disgust, but with disappointment. Hopes had been raised, which the new knowledge dashed.

There was always the possibility, of course, that Jeremy's story was some kind of elaborate joke. The boy's regard for truth had never been markedly strong, and, as the years passed, he showed no signs of being less anxious to draw attention to himself. But if he were lying, it still had to be explained how he had heard of her visit to Fish Square with Pimlico. And it was such a very *odd* claim to make if there was no substance in it.

Evelyn was not particularly keen on explaining human nature to herself. Explanations so often turned out to be wrong. People were so often guided by emotions that she had never experienced, and could not imagine experiencing. What made people choose to be terrorists? or nuns? or undertakers? A species capable of such aberrations was capable of anything. There was no accounting for their behaviour. But this revelation, or yarn, or fantasy, aroused her keenest curiosity. She could almost see, for the first time in her life, why her mother found people so endlessly fascinating, and talked about them all the time.

She caught her reflection in the glass of the case in which Royal Derby Ware was exhibited. She saw a very round, white face, fringed with dark red hair; a long neck and sloping shoulders. There was something extremely charming in her appearance; it was, she fancied, the kind of charm people call *gamine*. Jeremy stood by her, holding his chin and looking sagely at a piece of porcelain. His large, startlingly glossy brown eyes, and his hair, truly golden, were striking features. But otherwise they were much the same physical type. They both resembled unmistakably Lady Tradescant.

They held hands on their way out of the museum. Heads of passers-by turned to watch them.

The weekend was, as she had so much hoped it would be, a success. They spent the evening after their visit to the museum having a slow meal in Evelyn's favourite Italian restaurant. She felt enormously happy in his company. The things which he had told her were puzzling; at some stage, she would certainly have to find answers to them. But for the moment, she was simply delighted to be out with someone young. So many days and evenings with Mr Gormann had made her almost take it for granted that her companion should be old. Jeremy was refreshingly, absurdly young. His eyes were bright with ignorance of life.

They talked about their parents; whether their father was happy and how their mother occupied herself. Evelyn was startled to find how little Jeremy had begun to consider his parents as people. She forgot that she had only found this simple phenomenon out for herself very recently.

They talked about Oxford; how much Jeremy enjoyed it; how sad he would be to go down. She felt very nostalgic for her own, very recent, undergraduate days.

When they got back to the flat, Evelyn made up a camp bed in the sitting-room.

"There are no sheets or anything. I hope you don't mind."

"Course not."

"You can use the cushions on the sofa as pillows if you like."

"I'll be all right, really, sis. Got any more cigarettes, by the way?"

She offered him one from a packet that she had bought at the restaurant; they were French. She lit one for herself too.

"I wish I could tell you a bit more about me and Pimlico."

"It's all been a bit surprising, that's all."

"I can see that. I thought you must know."

"How could I know? Pimlico would never tell me a thing like that."

"I mean, that I'm gay."

"I thought that that was what you meant."

"I thought I'd grow out of it when I left school. Practically everyone did it there." He smoked ponderously. It was as if he felt he owed her an explanation.

"It must be awful." She did not know what to say.

"What's awful about it? It's no more awful than any other entanglement, I suppose."

"Except that it's different."

"I'm in love, Evie," he said suddenly. "Really in love. And I don't know what to do about it."

"With a man?"

"We're in the same year at Magdalen. I don't think he realises that I'm in love with him. It's terrible."

"Is he fond of you at all?" They had never shared information of this kind before. She did not know what to make of it, what to say.

"He's engaged to some girl or another. She's rather nice, actually. But I'm totally infatuated with him. I long for him. Do you know what I mean?"

"I don't think I do. I wish I did."

"You don't mind me telling you all this, do you?"

"All what? You haven't told me anything yet."

"Well, he's called Gordon. Gordon Smith, and he's reading English and he has a job fixed up in London for next year . . ."

"Publishing?"

"How did you know? And he's getting married in August. We play squash together sometimes. We get on very well, you understand. And I just don't know how to live with it all. I can't very well ask him to come to bed with me, can I?"

"No," admitted his elder sister. "You can't."

"What would you do?"

"If I was wildly and madly in love?"

"Mmm."

"I don't know." She yawned.

"See you in the morning, Evie. Thanks for listening."

They rose late the next day. It was half-way through "The Archers" when Evelyn woke up. Jeremy was still snoring when it ended. She went into the sitting-room and looked at him asleep. She was touched that he had chosen to confide in her. She could not decide whether to tell him that being in love when still an undergraduate is not something which ever lasts. It's like the crazes for religion or sport that some people go through when they're up. But she decided to let him find out for himself. He would have gone down in a few months.

She said his name. But he did not wake.

She shook him by the shoulders.

"Wake up!"

He groaned.

"Wake up, or I shall strip the bed!"

He lay impassively.

She tugged back the blankets with a girlish enthusiasm which recalled pillow fights and midnight feasts. A dormitory gesture. He lay, totally naked, and motionless. Then he opened his eyes and smiled.

She was chiefly struck by the size of it. Geoffrey's had always seemed a bit bent and shrivelled, and her not quite liking to mention her distaste for it had been one of the more awkward aspects of their relationship.

She just said, "Do you always sleep like this?"

"Yes. But I forgot my pyjamas."

Before she quite knew what was happening, she was reaching out. Jeremy giggled a little but made no motion.

"Never seen one of those before?"

"Not such a nice one."

"Family pride dear."

"Shall I undress too?"

She did not wait for an answer. He watched, his face still creased with laughter, as she took off her dressing-gown and pyjamas. Her pyjama jacket stuck as she pulled it over her head; and, while she struggled with buttons she felt Jeremy's hands covering her breasts.

Startled for a moment, they looked into one another's eyes. Then she lay down on him and fixed his lips with a kiss. Pleasure tingled through her body of a kind never felt with any other lover. A release of all the longings of the last months flooded upon her.

"How very Egyptian," Jeremy remarked after about half an hour had elapsed.

"And you presumably want breakfast."

By the time Jeremy had stirred himself properly and dressed himself, it was more like lunchtime. They ate a somewhat Scandinavian collation of cold meats with coffee.

Then they went out for a stroll in the Park. They did not speak about what had happened. They hardly spoke at all. Whatever had taken possession of them had stunned even Jeremy into silence.

Then, at about three o'clock, he announced his intention of going to church. Evelyn was dimly aware that he did have this side to his life, but she thought it very odd that he should express his intention of going to a Catholic service. He said it was a waste, living just behind the Oratory, and not going to Benediction.

She accompanied him. It was a strange sort of service, quite unlike the ones she sometimes went to with her parents in the village church at home. For one thing, nobody stood at the door giving out hymn-books as you went in. Everyone seemed to know the hymns, which were in Latin.

The climax of the ceremony appeared to be when, amid clouds of incense, the priest held up what looked like a rather elaborate mantelpiece clock and everyone, who was kneeling already, bent over even further. Jeremy just gazed at the object, in a rather soupy way, she thought. It was all most remarkably pagan and strange.

Jeremy was still quiet for a few moments after the service, but he cheered up when she suggested skipping tea and going straight on to drinks. The "booze" mentioned on his postcard had somehow failed to materialise, but she had some gin.

They ate a cheap supper in Earl's Court. It seemed a waste, when they had so much cold meat left in the fridge. But they felt festive. And after supper, she accompanied Jeremy back to Paddington.

It had all been a success. But it had also been a puzzle. She felt no nearer to knowing anyone. But on top of all the other puzzles, her brother had also become mysterious. Going to Catholic services was so very uncalled-for. To say nothing of the curious fact that he was, or had been, Pimlico's lover.

The thing she most wanted to know on that front was when it had last happened. Jeremy was so vague about it. She really knew less about it than if he had not mentioned it at all.

She had known Jeremy all her life. She could clearly remember having a bath with him, and what he looked like in the bath as a boy of four. That was what had been so magnificent when she stripped the bed. They had shared so many secrets which they had assumed they could keep hidden from their mother. Their existence had been something which each had taken for granted for as long as they could remember.

This is the mistake families make, she thought. They might know you quite well when you're ten; they assume that you're the same person when you're twelve, or fifteen, or twenty-five. They forget how much they are changing themselves. This was certainly true of her own relations with Jeremy. She felt, when he was a boy of about fifteen, that she had "got" him more or less right. They shared a lot of confidences. She had just left school and was in her first year at Newnham, and he would sometimes come to stay in Cambridge, feeling very grown up and looking almost infantile. They shared things then. She had no emotional life to speak of, and nor did he. They spoke without reserve about their passions and interests. She realised now that she had gone on with a picture in her mind of Jeremy as he was then. Whenever new data came forward, such as his turning out to be passionately interested in Pottery and Porcelain, or his failing Maths "O" level twice, she would slot this data into the pre-existent picture. She should have scrapped the old picture and started with a new one on each occasion. He could not be a young schoolboy with whom she enjoyed solving mathematical puzzles, and a slightly older schoolboy who was no good at maths. He could not be someone who was fond of football, who also happened to get into fearful trouble every term with his housemaster because he so consistently missed games. He could not now be a gorgeously flamboyant heterosexual, who also went to bed with middle-aged men of business. Or could he? There, the picture was blurred and distorted, and she knew the answer to none of her questions.

It still puzzled her that Mr Gormann should have a part in this world. Actually, she thought that Jeremy's assumption that Mr Gormann was "roughly speaking" a queer was facile. They met for tea the next day in the old man's flat at Fish Square.

While he was fussing with cups and lemons, her eye once more darted round the room for clues about his sexual identity. Whether he had been a supporter of the Nazis now seemed of infinitely less importance than whether the brown felt slippers with tartan linings, tucked under the writing-table, were the slippers of an entirely manly man.

"And how are the little ones?" he asked her, handing her a cup of tea.

"All right," she said. "One could do with less of the little ones and more of the bigger ones. *They're* taking exams this term, so they're all terrified and silent."

"Teachers always regard silence in children as a virtue. My own teachers were the same. I remember an extremely intelligent history master at the academy where I was reared – he was a Prussian with that fierce jaw and unyielding mouth. He struck us with a stick if we so much as opened our mouths in his lessons. How children are supposed to learn if they are not allowed to talk, I have always been at a loss to understand. We are not truly wise until we have learned to be articulate."

"If you ever tried teaching, you would ask yourself how children were ever supposed to learn if they all talked at once," she said, slightly snappily.

He smiled benignly. "I have wounded some professional pride.

Forgive me."

Tea was dispensed into delicate bone china cups and there were Ginger Nuts to eat.

"Jeremy came for the weekend. I think I told you."

"Your charming brother?"

"Whom you know."

"That would be an exaggeration. I have, shall we say, met him more than once."

"And," her voice trembled, "you never thought of mentioning it to me?"

"You are upset. I can tell you are upset, and yet I fail to see why. You must forgive me, my dear. Have I gravely offended?" His voice was kind and gentle.

"I just think it's a bit funny, that's all, that I've seen you almost every day for the last month or so and you haven't acknowledged that you know my brother."

A protesting hand went up.

"All right, then, that you've *met* him. Pimlico *knows* him I gather. John Price."

She could feel herself blushing. It was possible that this new boldness was a mistake. It might alienate the old man for ever. She had been warned not to press him with questions.

"You must know how fond I am of John," he said. "I am worried about him. But I owe you a confession. I must confess that after our first delightful meeting in Kensington Gardens, I told John about you and he said that you must be — what is the boy's name?"

"Jeremy."

"Precisely. That you must be Jeremy's sister. I do not know how well John knows Jeremy. He seems to have such a large circle of young friends, and I only meet the people he wants me to meet, of course. I never know how he finds them all. Do you?" He leaned forward on his chair suddenly.

"No."

"One is so terribly afraid that he will be unwise. I must confess to you what I have to confess though. It's this. i thought that if I got to know you, it might be a way of finding out more about John. Not spying, you understand. I thought that you might know . . . But I don't know now what it is that I would have expected you to know. It is an ungracious thing to say. It was, I repeat, only my intention *at first*. Since, very different considerations have entered into the matter. But there was a little deceit about the way I first came to know you. It is as well to make a clean breast of it, perhaps, since you appear to have knowledge of it already."

"Oh no, no, I did not mean . . ." She heard her voice trembling with emotion. He had been saying something very difficult. She stood up and took him by the hands.

"I am sorry to pry," she said. "I'm a nosey parker."

"What tiny and beautiful hands you have," he said, stroking her fingers.

She knelt down and put her head on his knees.

"I do love you," she said.

"Come."

He drew her up and sat her down on his lap in a paternal gesture. She snuggled up tightly in his arms. His lips gently touched her forehead.

"I do not want you to be hurt," he murmured into her hair. "I am so terribly afraid that you will be hurt."

"I don't mind being hurt," she sighed, nuzzling against his waistcoat. "Please hurt me as much as you like."

"What lovely hair you have."

She looked up into his face. Veins stood out in his neck and forehead. He was trembling. She kissed him on the lips and put her tongue into his mouth. The beard, which looked so wonderfully white and smooth, felt sharp and bristly against her face. They remained in one another's arms for a long time.

Later in the week, in Pimlico's flat, a surprising opportunity arose to bring some of her worries to the surface. She was, as a matter of fact, slightly worried about her behaviour with Mr Gormann. She had lost control, she told herself, and said things she did not mean. What she had done had given her physical pleasure. But it had not helped. She had gone to see Mr Gormann determined to bring things to light. She had actually plunged things into greater confusion. She had even interrupted Mr Gormann's explanation of why he pursued his friendship with her after their first meeting in Kensington Gardens. And nothing had been made clearer about Pimlico and Jeremy.

Pimlico's flat was decorated in the worst "Contemp" manner, redolent of his beloved fifties. Three of the walls in his sitting-room were painted green, and another was papered garishly orange. There were low-slung sofas and no overhead light.

"I'm worried about Theo," said Pimlico, gulping whisky.

"He looks all right to me."

"You've only known him a few weeks. How can you possibly tell?"

"True. How long have you known him?"

"Twenty-five years perhaps. I was doing National Service at the time. It's too long ago to remember."

"And were you Ban the Bomb too?"

"Lord, no. We met at a party or something. All Theo's friends are pick-ups. You will learn this eventually. Your own introduction to him, or lack of it, was entirely characteristic."

She laughed.

"Needless to say," he continued, "I'm terribly glad you did bump into him like that. It's awfully nice meeting up with you again. Theo told me he'd met you that first day. You can probably imagine it. You know how he talks about his friends."

"I suppose he does."

"I realised it must be you more or less at once, of course, having met you once or twice with Geoffrey. Who has broken his leg, by the way."

"So I heard."

"Oh, really. Who from?"

"Geoffrey himself."

"I say, how jolly nice."

88

"Was it?"

"I don't know. One doesn't know how other people's lives are arranged, after all."

"No, I suppose not."

"I mean, I wouldn't want to trespass on dear old Geoffrey's patch."

"How *do* you mean?"

"I mean that I wouldn't want Geoffrey to be jealous that I am entertaining his lady love in the evenings in my apartments."

"There is no reason for him to be jealous," said Evelyn coyly. "Anyway, its all been over between Geoffrey and me for a long time."

"So one had gathered somehow."

"We never really loved each other much." It astonished her to hear the words fall from her lips. Where had she got all this bilge-water about loving people from anyway? She suddenly had a horrible feeling that Pimlico was about to become soupy. She could not have borne it. She put on a crisp tone of voice and said, "I don't see any reason why you should be worried about Mr Gormann. He is very comfortable. He has plenty of friends."

"I don't think you realise how important you are becoming to him. I know I've said all this to you before. I just want to warn you, that's all. Theo is a terribly demanding friend. I've had over twenty years of it. I'm more or less hardened to it. He pursues his friendships very hard. They become absolutely everything to him. He is very selfish about it, I'm afraid."

"How do you mean?"

"He expects one to be available to him all the time, and at his own convenience. Damn it, he's got nothing to do all day. You'd think he might arrange his days to suit his friends, not expect them to fall in with his arrangements. I've been rung up in Stockholm at two o'clock in the morning before now. In the middle of important business trips. Just for a little chat, he says."

Pimlico Price filled his own glass and Evelyn's once more. She only gradually realised that he was very angry, not with her, but with Mr Gormann.

"People think because he has a white beard and a foreign accent, he is some dear old thing like Father Bloody Christmas."

He swigged some more whisky.

"He is not a dear old man. As a matter of fact, he is a very wicked, scheming old man. I hope that you realise that, Evelyn. He is an extremely powerful person. He can manipulate people. He knows all the tricks. He has been manipulating people all his life."

"Perhaps people like being manipulated."

Almost dangerously red and angry, he entirely missed her frivolous tone.

"You are absolutely right. They like being manipulated. But only into positions which they would have chosen anyway. And then they find themselves being pushed into doing something which they like doing rather less."

"I'm afraid that I don't know what you are talking about." She spoke quietly. She did not become angry easily herself, and it always disturbed her to see anger in others.

Her stillness calmed him down.

"I'm sorry," he said, "I shouldn't have spoken, perhaps."

"But now I want to hear. I want to know why Mr Gormann is a wicked man. I do not know him all that intimately. I've only known him a few weeks after all. I've never noticed anything wicked about his behaviour."

"All right. I will tell you." He crossed his legs and she observed an elegant ankle, chastely swathed in a long grey woollen sock. "Since you force me to tell you, I will tell you."

There had been no force applied by Evelyn of any kind. And she realised as he said the words that he had invited her there simply in order to make her hate Mr Gormann. She wondered why. The only explanation which occurred to her was that he must have begun to fall in love with her himself. He was jealous. She found it mildly flattering. He was, in his way, an agreeable man physically, and she found him quite pleasant company. But this needless massacre of Mr Gormann's reputation was distasteful and distressing. She only half listened to the stories. They sounded too extreme to be believable.

"There was another occasion," he was saying. "A delightful married couple called Sonya and Lev; they were White Russians. Theo met them on a cruise along the coast of Norway one summer. The usual sort of thing. Complete strangers. He conceived a wild passion for Lev. He used to tell me, which I am sure is untrue, that Sonya nagged him, and kept him short of food. There was a stage when it seemed as if Lev ate all his meals in Fish Square. It was a clear case of deliberately alienating someone's affection for his wife. The marriage ended disastrously, of course. They had been perfectly happy until they went on that cruise and met Theo."

"How can you know?"

"It is true," he sounded reasonable. "We can't *know* what marriages are like. I dare say that even Sonya and Lev did not know what was happening at first. But what we do know is that Lev spent an increasing amount of time with Theo and less and less with his wife. Then one night, he went home to find she had taken an overdose of sleeping pills. She was dead, of course."

"How awful!"

Evelyn was touched deeply by this story. Pimlico's malice was having its effect. Allowing for his exaggerations, she saw a measure of truth in his accusations. Mr Gormann was very demanding.

"He has a tendency to take people up with great enthusiasm," Pimlico continued, "and then to 'drop' them again with equal suddenness."

"He hasn't dropped you."

"I'm his broker. I'm rather more useful to him than most of his friends."

"You aren't being very useful to him at the moment."

A wave of the whisky glass conceded the point. He reached forward for the bottle and tried to reach Evelyn's glass without standing up. She covered it with her hand, so he refilled his own. He did not bother to get up and add water to it.

"I remember a charming little woman called Christine. I can't remember her other name, but I remember that it was Christine. It was at the time of the Profumo scandal, and we all joked about his having a friend with the same name as the glorious Keeler. We called her the Blessed Virgin Keeler. They were inseparable for about three months. Some people even spoke of the possibility of their getting married. But I knew that was going rather far. She even persuaded him to go to Mass with her from time to time. You know he's Catholic?"

"I hadn't really thought about it."

"Well he is. Or was. Yes, the Blessed Virgin Keeler used to arrive at Fish Square on a Sunday morning, clutching a mantilla and off they went to High Mass at Westminster Cathedral. But it didn't last, of course. He suddenly grew bored. I don't know what it was. It *may* have been the piety of the woman. He always implied that she started begging money and that this made it impossible to see her. I don't see why it should have done. I'm quite prepared to lend money to my friends. Everyone liked her. She used to do French knitting for the lepers."

He paused, an expression of ludicrous earnestness coming over his face, as he allowed the information to sink in.

"What happened to her?"

"She may still be kicking around for all I know. But she turned up one Sunday at Fish Square to be told by one of those fierce females at Reception that Mr Gormann could not receive her any more. Not a word of explanation. I'm sure she never saw him again. She was terribly distressed. She even rang me up about half a dozen times to find out what had happened. And we used to hate each other, so it shows how desperate she was. He had let her fall in love with him, d'you see. He wanted it to happen, so that he could hurt her. That's what I mean when I say he's a wicked person."

Evelyn was silent. All this information was disturbing, above all, because she did not know what to do with it, or how Pimlico expected her to react. Was she supposed to promise never to go near the old man again? Or was Pimlico merely letting off steam? It was impossible to tell. Lolling opposite her, whisky in hand, he looked perfectly sane. But his account of Mr Gormann was so wildly different in emphasis from what hers would have been that she began to wonder whether he were not suffering from some form of delusion.

"Anyway," he added, "I've told you now, and you're warned. Don't come running to me and telling me that I never warned you."

His tone was odd. She could not quite make it out.

"Let's talk about something else," she said.

"Like what?"

"Jeremy?" In for a penny, in for a pound.

"What's the old sod been telling you? This is another thing about Theo, you see, Evelyn. He can't let his friends get on with their own lives. He has to gossip about them all the time."

"I haven't heard anything about it from Mr Gormann. Jeremy told me himself."

"Told you what?" A note of fear had crept into his voice.

"You know."

He shrugged somewhat meaninglessly.

"It's true, I suppose? My brother would not just make a thing like that up."

"Wouldn't he? I would have thought that that was just the sort of thing that Jiminy Cricket would get into his pretty little head."

"Jiminy Cricket? Is that what you call him? It's really very confusing, this double nomenclature. It's like having to learn the Latin names of beetles as well as the English ones. You're Pimlico Price, I gather."

"The bloody mark of Cain. Everywhere one goes, one is stamped 'Fish Square'."

"Are you?"

"You've been having a nice little chat with someone, I can see. You want to get a confession out of me, don't you? A nice grisly confession. I can see why you and Theo are such pals. You're a bloody manipulator yourself."

She could not suppress a smile of total satisfaction to be cast in this role.

"Well, we had better be fair." His voice was really very slurred with alcohol. "You tell me something, and then I'll tell you something about dear Jiminy."

"What do you want to know?"

"Have you and Theo been just friends, or is there something more to it?"

"Of course we've been just friends. What can you be thinking of?"

"Not so much as a kiss, or a pat on the botty?"

"Of course not, no."

His face suddenly relaxed. The wrinkles on his brows were smoothed. It was as if a great burden had been lifted from him.

"You can't know how pleased I am to hear that. Look here, I should never have said all this stuff . . . You see . . . I should hate to think of such a thing happening."

"Well, it hasn't happened." She was firm in her untruth. She saw no necessity to confide in him, although she was going to extract as many secrets from him as possible.

"Now you must tell me about Jeremy."

"There's nothing to tell. I made rather a fool of myself, that's all."

"How did you make a fool of yourself? Jeremy says that you and he were lovers."

She would not normally have been so bold; it must have been the whisky.

"I don't know how much you know about it."

"Very little. I want you to tell me."

She was not going to let him off lightly. She was, in a quiet way, angry with him for having blackened Mr Gormann's name. She wanted her own version of Mr Gormann. Other people's versions were tiresome and made her feel jealous.

"The truth is, Evelyn, I was rather sweet on your bro. After all,

Evelyn, he is a very beautiful thing. He is, Evelyn, isn't he?"

"Yes. What happened?"

"Well we met."

"At an Old Etonian dinner, I gather?"

Pimlico began to shake. His face was very red. She realised after a few moments that he was helpless with laughter.

"He told you that . . . Oh, it's rich. It's rich . . ."

"Not at an Old Boys' dinner?"

"As a matter of fact, we didn't even go to the same school. You don't seem to realise that I'm not quite in that drawer . . ." His voice trailed away into giggles once again.

"Our actual place of meeting was rather less salubrious," he eventually managed to say. "Modesty forbids me to mention where it was. I picked him up, as you might say. I seduced him."

"Where did you seduce him?"

"It sounds awfully naughty saying it to you. God, I must be pissed. You see, it only turned out afterwards that he was a friend of Dodo's and all that crowd. I thought it was all quite anonymous."

"So he came here?"

"Yes, here."

"In this flat?"

"We had it off on that sofa you're sitting on, if you must know."

"Good Lord."

"I knew you'd be shocked. Women never have any idea that men in their own families have any sex in them."

"And this happens regularly?"

"He came back one evening about a week later, but it didn't seem the same when we knew who we both were. He hasn't let me touch him since. He's got religion, I believe. Not that I've ever noticed *that* interfering with people's sex lives."

"Probably not. So this has only happened twice?"

"Look, I'm tired, I'm pissed. Let's stop all this cross-questioning, shall we?"

"Have you seen him since?"

"He's vaguely a friend of Dicky Evans's or Dodo's. You know, I suppose. I've vaguely bumped into him at their place before now. And he came to a party of mine once. I thought Theo and he could talk about theology."

"You amaze me."

"Oh yes, Theo enjoys saints' lives. The more improbable the better for his taste."

"But since when did Jeremy?"

"My dear, he talked about little else but religion the second time he came here."

"I find it all rather depressing, needless to say," she said, in tones based on those of her own father.

"I'm pissed," he repeated. "I've told you more than I should have done." He had loosened his tie and undone his top button so that she could see those strangely grey hairs on his chest once again. They were unlike the hair on his head. It was like an old man's beard, showing through his shirt.

"I hope you don't think any the worse of me because of all this," he said plaintively.

"I think very much the worse of you. I think you have behaved perfectly abominably. Jeremy is little more than a boy. If I wanted, I could make things extremely difficult for you. It is very nearly the sort of thing people sue each other for. You could probably go to prison. You could have done a few years ago, anyway."

"Oh, do stop."

"Do you expect me not to find it outrageous?"

"You didn't have to ask about it if you found it all so shocking."

"I like that! So, I'm the one to blame."

"Why does it have to be a matter for blame?"

"I see. Nobody can blame you for anything you do. You are above it. But poor old Mr Gormann is different. You can blame him for a lot of things."

"Theo has nothing to do with it."

"I'm glad to hear you say it, but I don't altogether believe you."

"I don't want a quarrel," he pleaded wearily. "I would do anything rather than quarrel with you."

It was an almost sexual moment. She saw in his watery brown almost doggy eyes that he was speaking the truth. Dominion had been achieved over him, and she was not altogether sure how she had done it. But, with the wary sense that this would one day be useful to her, she stored up the memory of that evening with the quiet detachment of the psychologist or the blackmailer.

6

Time passed. Evelyn found that she was seeing Pimlico Price and
Mr Gormann in more or less equal doses. But she never saw them
together. That had not happened since the evening at the swimming-pool in Fish Square. She wondered how much either man
knew that she saw of the other. She never told them herself. She
felt instinctively that neither of them would be pleased, and yet she
failed to analyse why this should be so. Without being able to
articulate her feelings on the matter, she knew, however, that she
was "coming between" a long-standing, if unsatisfactory friendship, and that her arrival in Mr Gormann's world had disturbed
his life and Pimlico's more than had been at first intended.

That *some* disturbance had been intended by Mr Gormann there
was no possibility of doubt. The bathe, at which he had presided
like an Emperor at a gladiatorial contest, had been contrived for a
purpose. Had he intended that she should fall in love with Pimlico
Price, or Pimlico Price with her? The latter possibility, she questioned strongly. It would be impossible to know Pimlico Price for
twenty years and expect to "catch" him with a young lady.

Or would it? Jeremy implied in his sensational way that they
were all "at it", the men in Mr Gormann's world. And, now she
came to think about it, it was striking that she was the only

woman who was ever of the party at Fish Square. Mr Gormann *spoke* of other women; lunched with them; saved Chelsea and Wandsworth with them. But he did not introduce them to her. Pimlico, for all his whimsical talk about the feminine anatomy, did not appear to have any women in tow. Nevertheless, she thought it conceivable that Mr Gormann thought his friend to be as "normal", if less vulgarly so, as the legendary Pimlico of whom she had heard when still at University. He sometimes said, quite by the way, and with no emphasis, that "when John got married", this or that might occur. She had no sense that he intended, by this, to throw her together with Pimlico.

Whatever manipulations of her affection had been intended over the last few months, it was for Mr Gormann himself that she had come to long in a physical and passionate way. She had done no more than to curl up in his arms and be cuddled like a young child again. This was something, but she craved for more. In his presence, she felt an overpowering erotic attraction, so strong as to feel like the effects of some heavy drug. But, even so, there were other longings and desires mingled with the physical ones which she found equally baffling.

She was almost scared by her desire to dominate the two men; more, by the discovery that, in some areas, she was already able to do so. Mr Gormann, whom she had begun to suspect of being a manipulator of human characters in the circle which he had created about him, seemed himself able to be manipulated. She did not know where it would lead; but she did know, that if Pimlico were to discover the half of it, he would be angry.

The consequences of his anger, she saw to be a conflict in which he would either be lost to her, or in which she herself would be excluded from the circle altogether. Again, she was puzzled by having such thoughts, for she was not absolutely sure what she meant by them. She did not have a conscious desire to marry Pimlico, or even to become his mistress. The only conscious thought she had in his regard was a protective desire to keep him away from Jeremy. Yet, however vaguely articulated, she had a forceful sense that Pimlico Price must be hers, and that she must in some sense try to possess him. In part, she felt an awakening of that aspiration which had so thrilled her on her first encounter with Mr Gormann, intimations that life was to be different and, above everything, more comfortable.

Since becoming acquainted with the older man, she had come to share his obsession with the younger. There was, as Mr Gormann so often said about Pimlico Price, a wall of glass about the man. He was impenetrable. She herself was no adept at the emotional life. Geoffrey's parting had made her realise not only that she did not love Geoffrey, but that "falling in love" was not part of her repertoire. She had no experience of it, and something told her that she would never do so. This was a fact about herself which she guarded as a dear and wicked secret, locked like a monstrous child in the darker corners of some Gothic castle. It had often made her sad. But now she saw that it also made her safe; and, because safe, powerful.

Pimlico Price was, perhaps, also such a person. She had thought so at first. But she had changed her mind. One can recognise kindred spirits after a certain amount of contact, and he was decidedly not one. He had loved, perhaps still did love, passionately. She had questioned him the other evening as they sat together in his flat in Sloane Street.

"You needn't worry," she had added, as she saw his face tighten with worry. "I do not mean that I am in love with you, or expect you to be in love with me; now or ever. I merely wondered if you were in love with anyone. Jeremy, for instance."

"I've been sweet on Jeremy."

"That's not quite the same thing."

"I know. But I've been *pretty* sweet on Jeremy."

"And are you still?"

"A little bit."

They laughed.

She realised then, without being able to say why, that there was, or had been, a great love in Pimlico's life. But who the love *was* —

that was as incomprehensible as what the *life* had been. He was swathed in mystery. Even for Mr Gormann, who had known him for more than twenty years, he was opaque. It all came back to this business of whether human beings could ever really *know* each other.

"Getting to know John is like Robert Bruce's spider," he had enunciated one day to her amusement. It was the first concession he had made to entymological interest in their conversations. "The little creature tried, and tried and tried again, I believe. And that is what I have been doing these twenty years with John. Just when I believe the code to have been cracked, he eludes me once more. I have come to the conclusion that he must be a man to whom nobody matters in the slightest degree."

She had followed this clue, but it had got her nowhere. Work, evidently, was important; every so often he would disappear to "see to things in Scotland", but he never answered any questions about it on his return. He was thought to have a mother of bourgeois Presbyterian virtue.

He often complained about his work in the City and said that he would like to give it up. She moaned about her job, too. But she knew that the difference between them was that she would *really* have liked to give hers up. He would not. She was fairly sure that Scotland did not preoccupy him in the emotional way that she suspected someone or something in the world did, or had been able to do. He never spoke about his estates and lochs. There was no dreamy, far-away look in his eyes if salmon or haggis were mentioned. But he seemed like a broken, almost a love-lorn man, and, if Mr Gormann had noticed it too, it could not have been mere fancy on her part.

She also had to fit into her picture of Pimlico his warnings and assurances to her about Mr Gormann. He had, admittedly, been drinking a good deal when he made the most damaging of the assertions about his old friend. Evidently, his accounts of Mr Gormann's bad behaviour had elements of truth in them. From the pattern of her own friendship with Mr Gormann, she could see that he was demanding, that he was indiscreet, that he was capricious, and that he enjoyed taking up new friends at whim. There was the permanent danger that one might be dropped as suddenly as one had been taken up. These things she could see. But they did not, in her reading of events, justify the intensity of Pimlico's admonition to her. He had seemed not so much to be imparting information to her as trying to force her away from the old man. It was as if she were on the point of falling into a trap. The only explanation of this that she could think of was that Pimlico sensed, rightly, that about half her talk with Mr Gormann these days was taken up with the mysteriousness of his, Pimlico's, character.

Even his age foxed her. His memories dated him, or they would have done, if they had not been so self-consciously produced. He must have been in his very early forties, though his patches of grey hair made him seem older, and his behaviour made him seem as young as Jeremy. His years, like everything else about him, were indeterminate. One could not quite imagine *how he got there*. He sometimes spoke about his mother, evidently still alive and living near his "place" in Scotland. But such details as family life or childhood were impossible to reconstruct. Mr Gormann shed no light on these imponderables. He had met Pimlico's mother once, when she came to town. He could not much remember her, except that she had been formidable. John had been embarrassed and awkward at the time and the meeting had not lasted long.

He disliked, an habitual adage, parties *à trois*.

He was never still. She would see him one day; thirty-six hours later he would inform her that he had been to Zurich and back by air, or to Oxford. These visits to Oxford seemed fairly frequent. He had friends there with whom he stayed on Boars Hill. But she was never told their names. If she asked if he had seen Jeremy he would always reply elusively, sometimes shrugging and asking why it should matter, sometimes accusing her of being suspicious, sometimes admitting that he had seen the boy, but asking why this should be of any consequence.

She had come to decide that his assertion that he had only

made love twice to the boy was actually untrue, but she had no evidence to go on, and she was not sure how regular these interviews might be.

More than ever, she found the genius of Darwin consoling, one articulate voice to be heard through a Babel of sound, an island of sanity in an ocean of madness. One evening, instead of Mr Gormann reading poetry to her, as he often did, she read to him from *The Origin of Species*. So much of it seemed to be mere observation, mere common sense. But it was brightened by a luminous imagination which made her breathless with wonder as she read the unpretentious prose.

"The theory of natural selection is grounded on the belief that each new species is produced and maintained by having some advantage over those with whom it comes into competition; and the consequent extinction of the less favoured forms almost inevitably follows . . . The appearance of new forms and the disappearance of old forms, both those naturally and artificially produced, are bound together . . ."

She stopped reading for a moment and looked at him. He sat peacefully opposite her in a green velvet smoking jacket, a cigarette hanging loosely between his fingers.

"Come, child, and sit beside me," he said, "this reads too much like life."

"I'm not sure I know what you mean," she said in the rather arch tones which she used for teasing him. She came over and sat on his lap and fondled his hair with her fingers.

"I mean that this savage process of *selection* is what dogs our lives. We cannot be all to all. And I find myself only able to be all to one."

She trembled lightly as he held her.

"You are very, very dear to me," he said, "and it troubles me to think I cannot keep this to myself. But I must tell you and hurt you with it all."

"It doesn't hurt me, dearest." She put her hand inside his jacket and stroked his shirt.

"It is this tiresome, most tiresome business of selection," he repeated. "How can I say all this to you *without* hurt? You have come to me as a great blessing. When you are old and grey and unlovely I hope you will have similar good fortune."

"What are you trying to tell me?"

"I have already told you most of what there is to tell. You see, I have grown to love you, and this makes everything so difficult. At first, I thought our friendship was a kind of game; a happy game, it was true, and one that suited my purposes. From all that John said, I thought you must know him. I wondered if you, perhaps, had belonged to a circle that found him less difficult, less opaque. I have looked, and looked, these twenty years, for someone who had penetrated the glass wall. And it was worth trying you, as I have tried others. But alas, for you too, he is a mystery."

"He is rather." She sighed. He was on to his hobby-horse.

"But you see what your uncanny processes of natural selection have done for me, do you not? With the arrival of the new species, the consequent extinction of the old ones inevitably follows, does it not? You have eclipsed John in my heart, and I fear he knows it."

"But, how?"

"There is something about me, my dearest, which you have perhaps guessed already, but which I want to be frank and tell you about."

She swallowed hard. She was not sure that she wanted yet more revelations. She was content with areas of Mr Gormann's life being cloaked in obscurity. She wanted to be protected from too much knowledge.

"I have thought a long time about it, but I feel that you should know," he said. "As I say, you have perhaps guessed already. It is that I am, how shall I say this, a very wealthy man."

She stared at him with an almost monstrous gladness.

"I am, as a matter of fact, very rich indeed. My dear, would you be so kind as to put a cigarette in this holder for me?"

Her hands trembled as she did so. She put the holder in his mouth and lit the cigarette.

"Thank you."

He inhaled silently.

"You must understand," he said, "that what I have to tell you is strictly confidential; and delicate."

"Of course." She tried to control the excitement in her voice.

"Quite a lot of my fortune is tied up with John. I have, over the years, made over a considerable fortune to him. I established him in the City, for instance. And recently, the family firm in Scotland has been in difficulty, and I have expended a good deal on that."

"Firm?"

"A toffee factory in Glasgow."

"But I thought that he had estates."

"Did he tell you that he had?"

"No."

"What a romantic, at heart, you are, dear girl. No. There are no estates to speak of. Mrs Price lives in a perfectly respectable suburban house, I gather. They have a large garden. His people were prosperous factory-owners. They make 'Chewies', you know. But John's extravagant ways and the general economic climate have made them a good deal less prosperous than they were. There have been times when he has thought that he might have had to leave London and go and supervise the making of 'Chewies' himself. Since his father died, he has paid a managing director to do it for him. But times are hard. He has been struggling lately to keep the thing afloat. You can see that this must be kept strictly between ourselves."

"Of course, of course."

"As I say, I've settled a lot of money on John. He has learnt a great deal about how money works, and in recent years he had even been able to help me with my financial affairs." Mr Gormann pronounced every syllable in *financial*, making the "c" soft. "Apart from areas of my wealth which I am unable to deal with as my own, I have left him everything in my will. He has been the person in the world that I have loved best. It seemed a sensible arrangement."

Evelyn felt her heart beating with dangerous urgency. It was knocking violently against the old man's chest.

"I say that I loved him best. But I have loved without understanding. And now, in the winter of life, I have found love and understanding, or at least a measure of it, I find that I want to make you, my dearest, as happy as I was to have made dear John. It is my proposal that my wealth should be divided equally between the two of you."

There was a long shocked silence. He smoked peacefully. His eyes glistened slightly, and she could not tell whether smoke was getting in his eyes, or whether he was finding the promptings of generosity emotionally stirring.

"Have you nothing to say to old Gormann in reply?"

There was a demand in the voice. A suggestion, almost transparent, that she was being trapped, or simply bought. But it was not entirely disagreeable.

"Theo, I don't know what to say."

The feeblest of rejoinders; but she had been stunned into giving him a name.

"It will, of course, take some considerable time to get things straight," he said, fondling her hair.

"And I am not quite sure how I am going to raise the matter with John. He helps me deal with all my financial affairs now, and he would have to be consulted, unless I can think of some way of getting round him."

"At least you are only considering reducing the species and not extinguishing it altogether."

"True, my dear. But he will be hurt. You make old Gormann feel like God to talk like that."

"You are God."

"Well, I think, my dear, that after the savagery of your favourite Victorian, I should like a little poetry."

He reached down a volume from the shelf behind his head and began to read from his beloved Yeats – the only poet, as he had said to her once before, who conveyed what it was like to be old and lose one's friends. He obviously rather liked the image of the "foolish passionate man" that Yeats presented of himself in old age.

Mr Gormann's friendship had provided Evelyn with almost none of the satisfactions usually expected from friendship with coevals. But it had helped her to shed inhibitions and made her realise that not all inhibitions are manifestly sexual. Something had been touched in her, a sensation for which thrill was too trivial a word.

Leaning back in his arms as the old man read aloud, she knew herself to be rich.

7

It never occurred to her to question Mr Gormann's wish to impart so much of his wealth to her. The desire seemed a natural one, half expected. Since her first visit to Fish Square, when she had begun to penetrate his unknown world, and to feel herself part of his unlikely *entourage*, she had been vaguely aware of the fact that he would enrich her. The important things that happen to us rarely come as a surprise. It is as if we are prepared for them by an inner knowledge. The same had been true of her scholarship to Newnham – which had come as such a shock to her teachers. And she had known as soon as she set eyes on Geoffrey that he would become her lover. A recognition of these things did not articulate itself into an elaborate belief in fate; it seemed too casual, too ordinary for that. But it infused her with a deep distrust of the activity generally described as "making decisions". With heady resignation, she rested in the satisfaction that decisions had been made for her, though by what tutelary intelligences, she hardly had the curiosity to inquire.

It did not matter that no details had materialised about the money – when it would come, how much it would be. Her confidence in its coming had reached the level of mystic certainty, and required no deliberate proofs or figures written on a piece of paper.

A similarly nonchalant response to Mr Gormann's financial transactions was not to be expected from Pimlico Price, who stood to lose considerable sums by this whim of the Fates. Evelyn had said nothing to him about it. Nor, indeed, did she discuss it at any length with the old man after he had first expounded his intentions. And it was unthinkable that the two men should have discussed it together.

Evelyn no longer had any idea how much the two men knew about her individual friendships with them both. She had a suspicion that the daily telephone calls, visits, late evenings that had characterised their friendship when she first came on the scene had been rather toned down. Apart from anything else, she could not see how Mr Gormann could spare the time for an intense friendship with them both. The "inevitable extinction" of Pimlico Price from his life had already begun. At first, if she spent an evening with Pimlico, she had had the rather thrilling sense that it would all get back to Mr Gormann. She was fairly sure now that it would not.

Evidence of how far Mr Gormann and Pimlico had drifted apart came some weeks later when Pimlico rang her up and suggested a lunchtime drink at the Bunch of Grapes, a pub he much favoured; "just behind Smithfield" as he had unhelpfully described it the first time they ever met there. It had the supreme advantage, from Pimlico's point of view, of being almost perpetually empty, at whatever time of day one went into the saloon. It was far enough away from the City to guarantee – if its scruffy and not unsmelly atmosphere had not done so already – that none of his associates from Threadneedle Street would be likely to drop in at lunchtime. Nevertheless, it took no time to get there by taxi, rush-hour traffic not passing near its environs.

It had, apparently, been a favourite haunt of his for years, and he always made it clear to his friends, in the way that he so inscrutably could, that they were not to make a habit of going to the place unless accompanied by him. "Dicky Evans calls it my confessional," he had once said to Evelyn. "The Bunch of Grapes is essentially a place for parties *à deux*."

Few people lived near the pub. Those who worked within walking distance of it – students from Bart's Hospital, and butchers from Smithfield Market – understandably frequented other, jollier inns when they downed the lugubriously similar tools of their respective trades. How the place kept going at all was inexplicable to Evelyn, but when she raised the matter once with Pimlico he had been merely taken aback, that slightly baffled, hurt look coming over his face. He had made a remark to the effect that it was a "good old-fashioned pub", professing, which was palpably untrue, that he did not have much of a taste for "anything fancy". The truth was, as she had come to see more closely since knowing both him and Mr Gormann, that he had no taste at all in anything which related to the look or smell of the external universe. After Geoffrey, who could be tiresomely aesthetic at times, the contrast seemed peculiarly marked. The correctness of his appearance, in such details as socks, had nothing to do with taste at all. It merely stemmed from conformity, barely conscious, to old-fashioned models; perhaps enforced, if she were to know the whole truth, by the strictness of an upbringing in Scotland.

When she got to the Bunch of Grapes, Pimlico was sitting in a corner with the *Financial Times* on his knee, and a port and lemon on the table in front of him. A portrait of Sir Winston Churchill hung behind his head. The distinctive smell of the place – something of stale meat mingled with tobacco – assailed her as she walked through the large saloon.

The clientele of the pub at half past twelve on a weekday invariably consisted of a hall porter from St Bartholomew's Hospital – changed into *mufti*, but with the trousers of his livery still betraying themselves beneath a brown raincoat; an old lady called Agnes, who drank brandies and milk stout at the bar in rhythmical succession; and a seedy-looking man, possibly Irish, whose chin was always at the same stage of unshavenness, showing signs neither of recent contact with a razor, nor of more than two or three days growth. Very occasionally, these three, spaced well about the saloon, were joined by others; but the place was always sparsely occupied at the best of times and the customers were unfailingly aged.

The Irish man nodded politely to her as she bought a glass of cider at the bar. It was one of the peculiarities of their friendship that Pimlico rarely bought her drinks. "Going Dutch" was what he called it, a phrase recalling outings on no money at all with boys in Cambridge when she was still an undergraduate.

"There you are," said Pimlico with nervous crossness as she sat down at his table.

"Sorry. Am I late?"

"No. But I've been here a bit and I wasn't sure whether you'd turn up."

"I said I'd come."

"Of course you said you'd come. I'm just a bit on edge probably."

They sipped their drinks in silence. She had never seen him in quite this mood before. He looked awful. She wanted to help him say what he had to say, but was lost for the right approach. Her immediate thought was that his old mother in Glasgow had finally died.

"There's something I want to talk about," he managed to say at last.

"Is everything all right with your mother?" Certain that this was the source of the trouble, she allowed the words to sound as tender as she could make them. The old woman had, perhaps, merely had a stroke, broken an ankle. There was no cause, perhaps, for acute concern. But she was not, she could tell from the way he spoke, actually dead.

"My mother? Whatever makes you ask that. I think she is all right. Yes."

"I just wondered."

"Do you often wonder about my mother?"

"Old ladies . . . you know. One *worries*." The justification for her surmise was inane. She recollected his once saying – or was it

Mr Gormann? – that old Mrs Price was "as tough as old boots".

"You worry about my mother?"

It seemed impossible to make such a claim; ridiculous to answer "yes;" possibly callous to say "no".

"You seem rather anxious. I thought perhaps your mother was ill."

"Good lord, no. How very extraordinary."

He gulped down the last of his port and lemon.

"Mother's as tough as old boots. Let me get you another drink."

"I beg your pardon?"

She was astonished.

"Cider was it?"

The opportunity seemed too rare to be worth missing, Pimlico standing her a drink. But her glass was still quite full and she did not feel able to drink very much.

"I'm all right, actually, this drink will do me fine."

He accepted her lack of thirst without question and went to the bar for another port and lemon. When he returned, he said, "There *is* something I want to talk to you about, actually. The fact is, that since Theo has gone so funny, I have nobody to talk to about matters of this kind."

"Funny?"

"Yes – you must have noticed it over the last few months."

"You forget how short a time I've known him."

Which particular aspect of Mr Gormann's nature was being singled out as "funny" on this occasion intrigued her. The dispassionate observer might have found him in general a rather peculiar person; but a friend of twenty years' standing – and of standing as intimate as Pimlico's – would be expected to have accustomed himself to the idiosyncrasies of speech, dress and habit which Mr Gormann affected.

"Stand-offish," Pimlico continued. "Of course, it's happened before over little things – the way he suddenly shuts up like a clam when one asks harmless questions. I remember once asking him how he was. 'Hullo, Theo, old man, how are you?' Automatic sort

112

of question, you know. He sat absolutely silently for about five minutes, and then just said, 'Yes.' "

"He was probably feeling a bit off colour."

"He must be very off colour at the moment."

"I haven't noticed it."

"You perhaps haven't seen much of him lately."

The assertion seemed innocent enough, not designed to provoke a confession that she saw him every day. Evelyn was surprised. She saw how sadly the intimacy between the two men must have lessened, for Pimlico to be so unaware of the old man's movements.

"You perhaps don't realise that Theo is an extremely astute judge of financial matters."

"I hadn't really thought about that side of his life."

"Exactly. Music, poetry, all that crap. Gossip about his friends. You'd never think it to hear him talk, sometimes. Actually, he is a wizard financially. Would it surprise you to know that he is one of the richest men in London?"

"Very much."

"Well, he is. Nearly all the family money was banked in Switzerland, d'you see, before the war. Still is. He is very rich indeed."

When Pimlico Price talked about money, some of the same reverence came into his voice which characterised her father's tone when dropping the names of the aristocracy. They were tones of unmistakable piety, total seriousness.

"Rich men are always being pestered, as you can probably imagine. Begging letters, confidence tricksters. Theo has some funny stories to tell about them. Look here, let's drink some whisky."

This time, she did not protest. He shuffled to the bar and returned with two large tumblers of Scotch. She wondered if he would ever steel himself to the revelation which he so evidently intended to make. And she began to fear that he was playing "cat and mouse" with her – that some severe admonishment would be delivered when he was sufficiently tanked up, an accusation that she was appropriating money which should by rights belong to him.

"You know the way old people go funny," he said, gulping his drink. His speech was becoming noticeably slurred. "Rich people, I mean. Suddenly turn round out of the blue and leave their money to a bloody cats' home or something of the sort."

"Mr Gormann isn't leaving his money to a cats' home is he?"

"Who told you that?"

"No one told me."

"That's the way rumours start. Funny, though. It was wills I wanted to talk about, as a matter of fact. Wonder what made you mention wills."

"You mentioned them."

"Old ladies leaving their money to cats' homes. Yes. You see, the point is, someone is getting at Theo, and I am going to find out who it is. I want you to help me."

She sipped her whisky and opened her eyes very wide.

"Bloody awkward. 'Cause I've got a bloody good idea who it is. Let's have another."

"Do you think we should?"

"Why not? Makes things easier. Got something I want to tell you, as a matter of fact."

When he had come back, bearing two more glasses of whisky, he drew his chair closer to hers and patted her hand, giving her a rather goofy smile as he did so.

"Helps having someone to talk to," he said. "I don't know what I'd do without someone to talk to. I'd drink myself blind."

"I'm not sure I can be much help."

"You're reasonably rich yourself. You have never had to worry about money. Probably never had very much to do with actually making money. What was your father — a bishop or something wasn't he?"

"He was an ambassador."

"Anyway, you don't think of life in financial terms."

The final statement was so very much the reverse of what was the case that she listened with absorption at his bland analysis of her interests and temperament. It was clearly the product of long contemplation of the matter, a studied opinion, based on a sober assessment of the "evidence" which had presented itself to him. His voice had begun to sound more sober. He had obviously plucked up enough courage to deliver himself of a set speech.

"And because all these things are true, you are the last person in the world who is going to know what it's like to want to get your hands on someone else's money."

"I can imagine what it feels like."

"That's where you're wrong." He patted her hand again. "I think you're an innocent in these matters. And because you're an innocent, it won't have occurred to you that some people hover round Theo like vultures waiting to see what they can get out of him."

"Really?"

"Yes. Now, as I say, he used to be very good at dealing with them. Too good, sometimes. You've probably never seen Theo being heavy-handed?"

"No."

"Someone *now* has got their finger on him. Touched a soft spot."

"What makes you say that?"

"Well, I'm Theo's executor, and his financial adviser. He consults me about everything — used to, at any rate. When to buy and sell shares and so forth. I won't bore you with the details."

"I wouldn't understand them anyway."

She thought, how eagerly we fall into adopting the roles which other people expect of us. Some people would call it lying, but it wasn't really. Yeats's masks came to mind.

"The other day I bumped into Patterson. Do you know Patterson?"

"No."

"Theo's solicitor. Nice chap. Comes from Northern Ireland, you know."

"What happened?"

"When I bumped into Patterson?"

"Yes."

"Wait. I'm coming to that. He said — I'm an executor of the will, d'you see — that he was in the process of drawing up this new will — 'new will', mark you, as if I knew all about it — and how complicated it was. Said I'd have to come over and help him out when it actually came to the details."

"What did you say?"

"I said I hadn't heard of any new will. That he must have made a mistake."

"But he hadn't?"

"Said Theo had decided to leave a good quantity of his money to someone all of a sudden, which would alter the 'whole balance of the will'. That means it would be a bloody big sum. I can tell you. I mean, a few thou' here or there — to you, say . . ."

"To *me*?"

"Yes. Don't look so surprised. I shouldn't wonder if Theo decides to leave you a little bit. It's a very generous will — the old one, I mean. Little bits and pieces to all his friends. Nightmare for the executors, of course. As I say, if it had just been a few thou' to someone he'd forgotten about, Patterson would probably not have mentioned it."

She gulped. It might still, she told herself, be an exercise contrived to extract a confession from her.

"No, Theo is settling a big sum on someone. Naturally, I mentioned it to him next time we met. Damn it, he's gone through phases of asking my advice before he cashes a postal order."

"What did you say to him?"

"I may have been a bit blunt. I put it to him straight."

Evelyn wondered if he considered himself to be indulging in "straight" talk at the moment.

"He was completely evasive: I've never known him quite like it. I said I understood him to be making new arrangements about his will. Would he like me to help him? Damn me, if he didn't say that he hadn't changed his will. That was just a quibble. The point is, he was *going to*. Might have done already by now. He didn't give anything away to me, though. Not a sausage."

"Perhaps the solicitor was mistaken."

"Patterson. I called on him the next day at his office. Theo had obviously got on to him pretty fast. He said he was sorry to be so indiscreet. Said he'd assumed I'd been in on it, so to speak. All the same, there was no excuse for being unprofessional. All that crap. Said there was no excuse for discussing his client's business with someone else. 'Bloody hell,' I said, 'I'm the executor.' But that doesn't make any difference apparently."

"It's like doctors," Evelyn stated, but realising that it would be impossible to change the subject. "I remember a girl at school once who got pregnant. And the housemistress got in a terrible tizz because she said the doctor should have warned everyone. But he was quite right, of course. He could have been struck off the roll, even if it was the headmistress that he had told, without the girl's permission."

"Course I know about all that," said Pimlico rather crossly. "Course professional conduct matters. I'd be the last person in the world to deny that. I just think Patterson might have told me *something*. After all, he'd already spilt the beans. Theo's hiding something. You don't know what this means to me."

"What does it mean?"

"Of course, he's an old friend, and it's very hurtful. Of course." His troubled, angry face, as he repeated "of course" seemed to suggest that the ties of friendship, like the restrictions of professional life, were something of which he had to keep reminding himself, rather than anything he had felt. As on earlier occasions with him, she had the impression that almost no "natural" feelings came naturally to him, such obligations as they imposed being forced uneasily into the mould of his own egotism.

"Of course it hurts when an old friend suddenly stops confiding in you. That's what I mean by Theo's being funny lately. I don't even know how he spends his time any more. He took up enough of mine when it suited him, God knows. But this is more than just hurtful. It's bloody ruinous."

"In what way?"

"This is all confidential, you understand; between ourselves, I mean."

"Naturally."

"I don't mean to sound untrusting. It's just important to get these things straight."

"Of course it is."

"I mean, what Patterson said to me shows that you can't be too careful."

She conceded the general wisdom of the remark.

"The point is, Theo was going to leave me an awful lot of money. God knows, I've earned it. And I was counting on that money. It's not just me. I have my business to think of. I have a business in Scotland. I've probably not mentioned it to you before."

"I think you mentioned it once."

"It's a factory." He said the word as if it was highly distasteful to him.

"What does it make?"

"Confectionery. Chiefly confectionery."

"Sweets?"

"That sort of thing. The point is, that factory is going through a pretty hard time at the moment. Everyone is. There's a recession on. We just need Theo's money to keep it afloat. It's as simple as that. No one is going to lend us the stuff. Small family firm. No assets. Without Theo's money, we should be in very serious danger of going into liquidation."

This prospect, for a factory responsible for the manufacture of "Chewies", was picturesque, summoning up pictures of brown sticky vats dissolving into a flood of sweetness. But Pimlico's face remained stony and grave.

"If someone takes a great slice of the money Theo has promised me, that firm may very well go bankrupt."

"Is there no chance of it being saved without it?"

"There's always *chance*. That isn't the point. Theo has assured me that he will give me money which, now, presumably, he won't. I think he might have explained to me what he was doing."

"Perhaps he will."

"I don't think it very likely. Someone has pulled a fast one. And I have a very shrewd suspicion who it is."

Evelyn felt her heart beating violently.

"Who do you think it is?"

There was a silence, in which he stared intently at her. For a moment, she felt convinced that the game was up. The Bunch of Grapes, she remembered, was Pimlico's confessional. He had been drawing out the conversation in order to torture her — a manifestation of sadomasochistic tendencies only to be expected in one of his bizarre tastes and predilections. Now, if he faced her with a question point blank, she would be obliged to confess. The liquidated "Chewies", the unemployed toffee-makers, the broken friendship between Pimlico and Mr Gormann were all her fault.

"This affects you personally, of course," said Pimlico placing a hand on hers. "You know what I am saying. This is something which affects you very directly, if you want it to."

"I . . . I never *asked* . . ."

"If, as I say, you want it to."

Their eyes met. As she stared at him blankly, she saw that he was trying to convey something to her. He was smiling guilelessly.

"The money is," he added, to make the point clearer, "as much yours as mine. If you want it to be, that is."

This approach was unexpected, a quiet, persuasive appeal to her better nature.

"I don't know what to say. You've said yourself I don't have a very financial sort of mind."

"You'd assess the question then on purely financial terms?" There was a boyish tone of banter in what he said, but he looked crestfallen. She began to feel that she had got hold of the wrong end of the stick. She could not see what direction the conversation was taking.

"Obviously, I mind about how you feel." It was a complete lie.

The thought of the money, expanses of it, making life restful and lazy and rich, deadened her sense of anyone's feelings.

"But . . . you have no feelings in the matter yourself?" He looked at her imploringly. The smell of his breath was deeply alcoholic. "I'm not asking you to be passionately in love with me, or anything. I'm not such a fool as that. I just thought that, after a year or so, I don't know . . ."

The force of his words as they trailed off only gradually occurred to her. She repeated them, unspoken, in her mind, turned them over to see what possible interpretation could be placed upon them apart from the meaning which they actually seemed to bear.

"You are asking me to marry you?"

"That was rather the idea."

"And you are worried that if someone — this person — gets Theo's money, I shall want to marry you less?"

"Not at all. I just wanted to consult you. Don't take things the wrong way, Evelyn, please. God knows, I've got enough on my plate at the moment."

Whether from shock, or the whisky, or both, she felt her head spinning. The proposal had come as a total surprise. It was true that, in a way hard to analyse, she had grown rather fond of Pimlico. At times, in the last few months, she had felt quite obsessed with him. The fondness had been almost incidental. She was fascinated by the coincidence, if it was a coincidence, that he should have been an intimate of both Jeremy and Mr Gormann. In himself, she had only a small interest. As Mr Gormann's *confidant*, he was fascinating, and as Jeremy's lover, Pimlico and she had in a grotesque way much in common. But she had no notion of how he could have formed the impression that she would make a suitable wife for him; beyond the obvious attraction that she was Jeremy's sister.

"I don't know what to say. That's all."

"You can't be surprised. I took long enough saying it."

"But I hadn't expected you to say it at all. I thought you'd asked me here to talk about Theo. I mean, I didn't know you wanted to get married at all. I'm putting all this hopelessly badly. But can I . . . Do you mind if I don't answer all at once? It's rather a shock, that's all." She drained her whisky.

"Of course, you must have time to think it out."

"You are sure that that's what you're really asking me?"

He patted her hand, and nodded at her.

Outside the pub, they strolled together as far as St Paul's Cathedral. It was hot, heavy weather, the sky quite bright to the south, but a furious dark cloud hovering over the great dome. Everyone had been saying all day that it was going to break.

London was full of tourists; ordinary traffic merely sandwiched between charabancs; everyone seeming to move about in crowds of not less than thirty, conducted by couriers speaking an alien tongue.

"I'm very, very fond of you. I just need time to think, that's all," said Evelyn, as they parted.

He squeezed her tightly on the steps of the cathedral. A few score of Germans paraded past them into the west porch. It was a clumsy sort of embrace. Something suddenly reminded her of Geoffrey.

8

Time to think was provided when, some days later, Pimlico left for Scotland. There was a crisis in the firm which required his attention and would take several weeks to sort out. He then intended to take a fishing-holiday with some business friends in the Trossachs. They both agreed that such a parting would be "good for them"; it appeared to fit in with some pre-conceived notion that Pimlico had of how potentially betrothed couples should conduct themselves.

Time to think, on the other hand, did not make it any easier to know what to think. After a good deal of search for more probable explanations, she had concluded that his proposal of marriage was sincere, based on an affectionate desire to make her his wife. More dubious motives had suggested themselves at first. If Pimlico had known that Evelyn was the new beneficiary of Mr Gormann's will, securing her as a marriage partner would have been a neat way of guaranteeing that the money would not pass out of his hands. But she could see no trace in his demeanour that he suspected anything of the kind. As far as she could surmise, piecing together various hints he had made, it seemed likely that he suspected Richard Evans of being the one who had, as he put it, "twisted Theo's arm."

Evelyn had only a shadowy sense of who Richard Evans was. Mr Gormann always spoke of him in the same breath as Dodo de Waal, who had been at Jeremy's college and now had some job in the art world. "Dicky Evans and David love the pool," Mr Gormann often said, when watching bathers at Fish Square. Richard Evans's imagined claims to the money were based, in so far as she could make it out, on disappointment in other quarters, a relative having recently died without leaving an expected legacy to him. Evans had confided all this to Pimlico in the saloon of the Bunch of Grapes and, from the way Pimlico related the matter, it was clear that he suspected his friend of trying to make Mr Gormann compensate for his misfortune. Dodo was also said to be a key card in the trick; but how, she did not know.

Pimlico's fantasies on this score were earnest enough to assure her that he had no inkling of her own expectations.

A more substantial doubt in her mind was whether he wanted to marry her for the sake of Jeremy. The difficulty of holding down homosexual liaisons was notorious: even she was aware of it. By marrying the loved one's sister, one might ensure, if the sister were reasonably close to the boy, that contact with him might be maintained. The complexity of this motive, if it existed, was probably unknown even to Pimlico himself. The thought of it got Evelyn nowhere.

She had not heard from Jeremy for some weeks. He had, presumably, sat his finals at Oxford. Letters from home suggested that Sir Derek had high hopes for the boy, and was expecting him to start at the Foreign Office in the autumn. Lady Tradescant's letters struck a more sober note, stressing the difficulty of the exams, how nervous Jeremy must be, how oppressive it was to work in the heat, and other observations which could be referred to at a later date to console the family, should the result be less good than was expected.

It would have been unlike Jeremy to write to Evelyn about his exams. But she was sorry to be out of touch with him; and pleased when the morning post brought an envelope decorated with his florid, rather large handwriting. There was also a typed airmail letter from Geoffrey; the third that week. These had been coming quite a lot lately, nagging reminders of the *persona* she had discarded before summer began. She tore it into tiny shreds without opening it before reading Jeremy's.

Dear Gordon,

she read.

I am sorry that you are so upset. I am, too, needless to say. After I finally managed to pluck up enough courage to tell you how much I loved you, I thought it would mean we could never speak to each other again. And then there was the knock at my door that evening, and it was you.

I'd come to think that the perfect sexual experience was impossible until that moment. But there you were, all beautiful six feet of you, wanting it as much as I did. It was the most wonderful evening of my life.

I don't believe it when you write that you were just coming back to pick up your squash racket; or that I pushed you into it.

Of course, I'm sorry about Brenda. But surely if human relationships can't stand up to people telling the truth to each other, they can't be very real, can they? Better for her to find out about you now than later, after you were married.

Let's get together again *soon*.

Love, (still!!!) J.

Compulsive reading, as letters not meant for oneself invariably are, it nevertheless disquieted her. She was irritated that the evening with Gordon, presumably recent, and since *her* weekend with her brother, had been the most perfect sexual experience of his life. The ingenious tone of the letter, its youthful solemnity, touched her, however; particularly its egotistical implication that

124

making a mess of Gordon's affairs for him was something which deserved a measure of thanks. She was young enough herself, perhaps all human beings are, to share her brother's preoccupation with the perfect sexual experience. It was the closest she came to mysticism. With men, she felt sure, it was different; so comically apparent when they were aroused by desire, so seemingly obvious when it was over, spurting out of them like milk boiling over in a saucepan. No fears for them, except in cases of absolute insanity, that they would become pregnant. No menstrual pains, so far as she knew, to upset them. She had tried to find out from Geoffrey whether it hurt at all; but had received no coherent explanation. Their pokers seemed so vulnerable, changing shape in an instant, now all large and proud, now soft and crestfallen: like their owners, all bluff, really. It must hurt a bit, sticking those things up us all the time, she thought. Her bush felt so very rough, even to her finger-tips.

Gratification in these areas proved elusive. The tumble with Jeremy had been exceptional, the first time for ages that she had really taken off and felt dizzy with excitement. With Geoffrey, these moments had been rare, even in the early days. He had been too quick, too much in a hurry to get the thing over, unaware, it seemed, that there could have been anything in it for her. He had not been her first lover. She lost her virginity in her first year at Newnham to a young man she hardly knew, called Arthur. They had been to see a Czechoslovakian film at the Arts cinema, during which he had skilfully managed to put his hand inside her knickers before she knew what he was up to. It had been flattering. She had gone back to his college rooms fairly eagerly. It was not as much fun as she had hoped, though. He seemed so fearfully business-like about it – carefully unwrapping his condom before he started. Then undressing her as she lay on the bed. Then taking off his own clothes and unrolling the thing on to that cock of his. And then folding his underpants before he started. It was all so slick. He had clearly done it dozens of times with dozens of girls. It hurt a lot too, that first time. He said, "Bloody Christ, you're a virgin," which, although she was irreligious, she had thought rather strong language. And she innocently wondered how he could tell.

They never did it again. At first, she thought that she would die as a result of it, possibly of venereal disease. Later, she became rather grateful to Arthur for having broken her in. Hers had been a promiscuous year. Proficiency in bed was rather expected of a girl, rather as needlework and music, or related accomplishments, had been expected of their great grandmothers.

She "went with" several young men during her second year. The most exotic of them was the son of an Arab oil magnate, with such a big one that she thought she would burst when it entered her. Then he had tried to persuade her to suck it, which she felt very disinclined to do. He had surprised her then by saying that his wife enjoyed doing so, but she still refused. Afterwards, she did not know whether the adultery — as it had turned out to be — or the presumably enormous wealth of the boy had been most exciting.

Then there had come a dull patch when she had really thought that she *was* lesbian. Memories of school had haunted her. But although quite willing to experiment again in that direction, nothing ever came of it. There was a nice girl in her corridor called Anna, who smoked a pipe. Evelyn had made particular overtures of friendship — inviting her to cocoa at bedtime, listening to her ghastly Wagner on the gramophone: to no effect. And then she had met Geoffrey.

If she were lesbian — she still did not rule out the possibility — this would presumably stem from some preoccupation with her father. Or so her slight reading of popular psychology would have suggested. The trouble was that she did not think she had very strong feelings about Sir Derek at all. Perhaps that was the trouble. Perhaps this explained the fascination of Mr Gormann.

Certainly, wherever gratification was to be found, she felt anxious for greater intimacies with the old man. Her memories of undergraduate *amours*, so vividly recalled by the tone of Jeremy's letter to his boy-friend, seemed impossibly slight when weighed against these new feelings which had come upon her since knowing Gormann. They had kissed, and he had seemed to like that. But he was so courtly, so comically noble, that she felt anxious about proceeding further without direct overtures from him. On a most practical level, she wondered what he was capable of, at his age. Again, she knew that men weren't the *same* as women – but how different they were, she had no notion. Perhaps actually to be fucked by the old gentleman would destroy something of the magic of their relationship, a removal of all masks being something alien to the very nature of the friendship since its dawning.

Now, Pimlico's proposal had come to complicate things. For a proposal of marriage, surely, included a proposal of bed. He was a handsome man. She was still haunted by the wonderfully thick, slightly greying hair on his chest, revealed at the swimming-bath in Fish Square. And in a way she found it hard to articulate, she *did* want to dominate him, perhaps an innately wifely desire, calling for his proposal as a natural consequence. But his kisses seemed so very clumsy, inept, that she felt that there was much for him to learn, and teaching someone whom she did not love would be no fun. Sex aside, she wondered how safe it would be to marry a man with such an obvious weakness for the bottle.

It slightly surprised her, as she washed up her breakfast, that she should have been considering marriage with Pimlico so seriously. But it is hard not to take flattery seriously, and any proposal of marriage is a tonic to the ego. She was still sufficiently unaware of what he was like to be fascinated by the wrongness of her first impressions of him. "Girl-friends" – "women", in Geoffrey's phrase – had been part of the original picture. Several of her friends had been actually named by Geoffrey as "Pimlico's women". She saw now that a certain obvious handsomeness of feature, combined with the ability to appear on a sufficient number of occasions in the company of the right sort of girl, confirmed the reputation for womanising which he had built up. A few bawdy heterosexual jokes lent weight to the picture. But actually, when people have once built up a reputation, of whatever kind, they do not need to work at it. Indeed, there will be little they can do to change it, in most circles. The man whose friends all attribute him with lack of promptness can turn up on time to every engagement in the year, but on the one occasion when he fails to do so, he will provoke the delighted response that his lapse is "just like him". Evelyn had noticed within herself a desire for people to act the parts which were expected of them, regardless of suitability. Perhaps it is the desire to look behind the mask, the belief that there is a more real character behind it which is itself spurious. But she felt anxious to know people, when marriage was in question.

She had said that she would give Mr Gormann tea in her flat that afternoon, but otherwise she had made no arrangements for her day. Putting Jeremy's letter in her handbag, she set out for the Natural History Museum, a few hundred yards down the road; the only place she knew which provided her with fresh preoccupations, and a refuge from self.

The insect gallery was not, actually, the best thing about it. Evelyn felt that it was a mistake to see beetles arranged in rows; and although she enjoyed individual exhibits, the Burying Beetle, feasting on a stuffed mouse, the Rose Chafers glowing like a pair of emerald earrings, she felt that the bigger beasts exhibited better. The *thought* of such great water creatures always interested her vastly less than the thought of insects and birds. She had none of the naturalist's interest in them. But an actual sight of them was different, magnificently impressive. The huge skeleton of the Greenland Right Whale in the Whale Hall, or the gaping crocodile in the Reptile Gallery filled her with almost religious awe.

She strolled around staring at them meditatively for some hours. Then she decided to visit Harrods and have an early lunch there. As she came down the staircase of the museum, the huge entrance hall, guarded by two majestic elephants, echoed to the din of school children. She gazed at the rhinoceros with one last longing look, and then walked out into the Cromwell Road.

She returned to her flat before two o'clock and found Jeremy pacing up and down the mews with an irritated expression on his face. He had had his hair cut quite short, so that it clung to his head in tight curls.

"What a nice surprise." She kissed him.

"I'd given up hope of finding you in. Didn't you get my letter?"

"Yes and no."

"Oh, fuck. Don't say I've done it again."

"Again?"

"I rang Gordon this morning, and he said he got a letter from me meant for Ma and Pa."

"I got one meant for him. Come on in."

She held the door open for him. He picked up the loose canvas bag in which he humped around his belongings and he went upstairs into the sitting room.

"You read it presumably?"

"I could hardly help it."

"So you know all there is to know."

"Not what you said in your letter to me."

She ran her fingers through his hair. He smiled nervously, avoiding her gaze.

"I like it shorter," she said.

"You can't have got my letter."

"No. That's been sent home, presumably. If Gordon got the one for Ma and Pa, and I got the one for Gordon, the one for me . . . unless there were more . . . You really ought to be more careful. Imagine if Ma and Pa saw what you wrote to Gordon."

"Christ, have you got a cigarette?" He sat down on the sofa. His face was quite pale.

"Horrid old English ones, as you call them." She held out a packet.

He puffed silently for a while.

"You don't think I did send it home, do you, sis?"

"Darling child, I don't know, do I? You put them in the envelopes. You posted them, presumably."

"I know, fuck it. I just can't remember. I did write another. I was sending off a cheque for my tickets."

"Well, perhaps Ma and Pa got the cheque."

"Perhaps."

"Would it make any difference if they did see the letter?"

"Depends what you call difference."

"What did it say?"

"That Gordon and I . . ."

"God, Jeremy, you *idiot* . . ."

"Wait for it. That Gordon and I were having a holiday together. That's what the cheque was for. For the tickets."

"That's innocent enough."

"And I said that in view of the fact that he and I are having a serious sexual – very sexual – relationship, I think you and I should be just, well, brother and sister again . . ."

"You wrote that in a *letter* . . ."

"I found it easier to write it down. It's difficult talking, God, these fags are foul. What make are they?"

She told him.

"Have a 'Chewy' to take the taste away."

"What are 'Chewies'? No thanks. Got another fag? Thanks." He lit up. "It isn't that I didn't *enjoy* what we did last time I came to stay. I don't want you to think that."

"Is this what you wrote, or what you're saying now?"

"Both. It was a really beautiful experience. Really. It was. I just don't feel I can keep two things going at once when one of them is as big as this thing with Gordon."

"I can't compete."

"Look, sis, what are we going to do? If Ma and Pa read that letter . . . you haven't heard the half of it yet."

"I haven't?"

"Not the worst bit."

"Our parents find out that their children are committing incest and that's not the worst bit?"

"There's no need to shriek. It's not the worst bit as far as Pa is concerned. I haven't got my degree."

"What?"

"I didn't just get a third, or a pass degree. I failed to get any kind of degree at all."

"But Ma wrote to me about a week ago saying you thought you'd done rather well."

"I know."

"They said you'd done rather well."

"I heard you. I was lying. I totally cocked up my Charlemagne paper. It was the first paper I did. My special subject. I just stared at the questions. I couldn't do a bloody one."

"Most people feel like that in exams."

"They didn't look like that. Scribbling away, the buggers. I just sat there. I honestly couldn't answer a single bloody thing."

"So, how did you do on the other papers?"

"I didn't sit any of the other papers. I just couldn't face it. I felt so ill. God, I was ill."

She stared at him, appalled. She felt shocked, helpless. Walking out of examinations was, in her scale of values, an unthinkable thing to do; so outrageous that she could not even begin to imagine doing it.

Colour was returning to Jeremy's face. He was, in fact, going very red. At first, she thought he was giggling; then she realised that he was in tears. She sat down next to him on the sofa and put her arm round him.

"I've really cocked things up, haven't I?"

"Rather."

"Utterly."

"Come on." She gave him a handkerchief, into which he blew his nose.

"Sorry."

"No need to be sorry." She did not mean it. She really felt cross with the boy: there was every reason for him to be sorry.

"Look, Jeremy, if Ma and Pa have read your letter, we're going to have to work out what to do. They aren't going to take it very well, you know."

"No."

"Now, what did you say, exactly?"

"God, I've told you, haven't I?"

"You said that you and Gordon were going on holiday. That you and I were lovers."

"Yes."

"And that you'd walked out of your exams. What else did you say?"

"I said that Gordon and I were going hitch-hiking across Europe – going to try to get to Istanbul. That I was going to split for a bit, have a break."

"You mean, not come back?"

"Just for a year or two. It was really asking you if you'd break the news to Ma and Pa. You see, I couldn't really face telling the truth about everything."

"No."

She was prevented from dwelling on the cool way in which Jeremy had expected her to help him out of his difficulties by breaking this unacceptable news to their parents, by the telephone ringing.

"Darling?"

"Hullo."

"Evelyn? Is that you? Ma here."

"Yes."

"How are you, darling?"

"Fine."

"Good. Your father and I were a bit worried. You haven't written for a while."

"Sorry."

"I know darling, you've been busy."

"A little bit."

"I know how busy you are. Look, darling, do you think there's any chance of my being able to pop in and see you this afternoon?"

"Well, I've someone coming to tea . . ."

"It's rather important. Something's cropped up. I'm sure it isn't anything really, but you know how your father worries."

"Where are you?"

"Just outside South Kensington Station."

"Good heavens, just round the corner."

"Yes. I thought I'd ring first, though. If it's awfully inconvenient, I can go shopping or something."

"Course it's not inconvenient, Ma. I just thought you were speaking from home, that's all."

"Your father thinks I'm in Aylesbury."

"Why does he think that?"

"I told him that that was where I was going."

Bleeping interrupted them, and then the line went dead.

"That was Ma. She'll be here in a minute."

"Christ. What are we going to say?"

"*We* aren't going to say anything. You had better wait in the bedroom until she's gone. I expect she wants a private talk with me."

"Had they got the letter?"

"Obviously."

"Did she say so?"

"Not in so many words."

"Great. Then perhaps they got my cheque for the tickets."

"Quick. Get in there." She shoved her brother into the bedroom; the door-bell was ringing.

"Coming!" she called out airily as she sauntered down the stairs. It was her playful, both-girls-together sort of voice, one she used to sweeten her mother in awkward moments. She flung open the door.

"You know Mr Binding," said Sir Derek.

Her father stood there, wearing a bowler hat. By his side was the vicar of the village church at home. She pecked her father on the cheek.

"How do you do," said the clergyman. "Your father brought me along."

"So I see."

"This was not a job for me to do alone," said Sir Derek, as he followed Evelyn upstairs. "Mr Binding very kindly offered to come. I couldn't, in the circumstances, bring your mother. I don't want her being upset."

"Quite proper," said Mr Binding.

"What is it?" Evelyn asked. "No one's ill, are they?" Wounded innocence was, she decided, the best attitude to affect. The impropriety of bringing the vicar was ridiculous; doubtless habit, based on a lifetime of discussing confidential diplomatic affairs in the presence of underlings and private secretaries.

"I'm just here to listen," said Mr Binding. "To listen, and, if I can, to help. There's not enough listening done by the world today, and all too often my profession are the cardinal offenders, I'm afraid."

"The fact is," said Sir Derek, with extreme diffidence, "your mother and I have had a letter from Jeremy."

"That's unusual."

"I don't think that this is an occasion when flippancy is in place."

"Sorry, Pa."

"Of course, we don't believe all the letter. It is quite clearly the product of a deranged mind. But I want you to tell me how much truth there is in it."

"I don't know. I haven't read it."

"I have it here. I should warn you that it is addressed to you. I needn't say, I think, Mr Binding, how sad I was that my wife had to read that letter."

"It is a very, very sad letter," agreed the parson.

Her father handed her the envelope. The letter contained, in substance, all the things that Jeremy had told her. It was unmistakable in its implications. Totally explicit. *I never knew that fucking a girl could be a really beautiful experience until we had it off together . . .* Her eye kept returning to the sentence.

"Of course, we rang up the college at once," said her father. "It's perfectly true, I'm afraid. He simply didn't sit the examination. I can't think what came over the boy. He had been working so well."

"Many people go through phases of being, shall we say, strongly attached to their own sex," said the vicar. "It's a perfectly natural, healthy phase, that's all." His manner suggested that contemplation of this phase was not unpleasurable; even, that the phase could last into later life without cause for disquiet. He had a nasty nasal twang to his voice and he spoke in quiet, clipped phrases. Nobody liked him in the village. He had recently come to the parish from Southend-on-Sea.

"What I can't get over," said Sir Derek, "is his lying about it. We've always been a very close family, able to talk about things. There'll be no chance of a Foreign Office job for him now."

"What I think is so significant," said the clergyman, contemplating his hands as if they were rather good Ming, "is that he addressed it to you, Evelyn — I may call you Evelyn? — you see, rather than to his parents. He obviously wanted his parents to see the letter, but he could not bring himself to address them directly. This is the nub of the question in my view."

"They'll never believe it at Eton, you know. His housemaster told me that Jeremy was one of the ablest boys he had ever taught. Simply couldn't understand the college not giving him a scholarship."

"The — er — what you might call *sexual* fantasies," pursued the clergyman, "are fairly closely bound up with his feelings for you, do you see. You probably weren't aware he was having them. People usually aren't. You were, as it were, the focus through which they were being channelled. But it would be very interesting if you could throw light on them."

The door bell rang. Evelyn, who had been sitting quietly while the two men spoke, as if to themselves, got up to answer it.

"Pa's here," they heard her say on the stairs.

"Your father? But he's spending the day with the vicar. Parish Council business. He told me so himself."

"They're both here."

"Lady Tradescant." The limp little clergyman had come down to greet her.

135

"Mr Binding. What a surprise to see you here. I didn't know you held your Parish Council Meetings in London."

The vicar muttered something about matters of some delicacy.

"Well, really, when you said you were going to Ayles-bury . . ." Sir Derek's usually waxy, slightly yellow face had darkened with anger when they returned to the sitting-room.

"Don't argue, dear, we're both as bad as each other. Well, darling," she turned to Evelyn, "it's all looking very nice. You've moved that chair. And the lamps."

"Just for the summer."

"They're nicer now. You know, I nearly got lost on my way from Marylebone. London's awful. They've knocked a new bit down every time I come."

Sir Derek's face had become quite impassive. What animation it had possessed a few moments before seemed to have vanished, as if something living had been frozen into a wax-work. The light from a standard lamp glistened in his steel-rimmed spectacles.

"This is most awkward," he said.

"It's not as awkward for us as it is for Evelyn," returned Lady Tradescant. "Have you told her what was in poor Jeremy's letter?"

"I've read it."

"I'd never seen the word written out before. Eff-ing, I mean. I saw it written on a wall once at the beginning of the war. I was with your Aunt Meg at the time. She had to explain to me what it meant. Even then I found it unbelievable. But this is . . . I mean, it's a criminal offence. You could go to prison."

Evelyn was not sure whether her mother meant that writing the *word* was criminal, or indulging in the activity it described with someone of too intimate kindred or affinity. It appeared that neither of her parents had considered it possible that the activity had really taken place. That was one consolation. But there was still the problem to be surmounted of how to get them all out of the flat without knowing that Jeremy was in her bedroom.

"Something must clearly be done," said Sir Derek. "The boy

must see a psychiatrist, as Mr Binding has said."

"Did you say that, vicar? How perfectly awful. I wouldn't want one of my children sent to a person of that kind. Your cousin Frances was sent to one, you know, darling. Perfectly ridiculous, she wasn't mad at all. And, of course, it cost Lily and Hugh a fortune. He just made her sit down and talk about sex all the time. Quite unsuitable."

"If I may put in a word," said the clergyman, "without speaking out of turn, it does seem to me that the letter shows definite traces of schizophrenia. Consider the simple fact that he wrote the letter to his sister, but addressed it to his parents. You see, as I see it, two Jeremys wrote that letter: the Jeremy who is Evelyn's brother – with all the frustrations and desires of the perfectly normal, healthy, highly-sexed young man" – he paused, a glint coming into his eyes as he spoke – "and the other Jeremy, the little boy who has made a mess of things, and wants to run home to Mummy and Daddy."

"I think Mr Binding is right," added Sir Derek, with an air, not of conviction, but of resignation; his view seemed to be coloured by the idea that it was right to leave anything so unpalatable as human character in the hands of the experts, however implausible their conclusions.

"You're all much cleverer than I am," said Lady Tradescant. Evelyn was proud that her mother was behaving with a sort of dignity and not thinking it necessary to pretend that she was not upset. "But if Jeremy wants to run home to us, why doesn't he do it? We have absolutely no idea where he is. That's why I've come to see you darling. He's likelier to have come to you than to us."

"*Do* you know where he is?" her father asked sharply. The question was bound to be raised sooner or later. A confession that he was in the bedroom would possibly lead to an embarrassing reassessment of the letter, particularly since, if she had had nothing to hide, she would have declared his presence at once. A lie, on the other hand, was equally liable to lead to difficulties, should her mother, as she usually did, ask if she could have "a poke round" the flat to see what furnishings had been altered.

A voice on the stairs prevented her answer.

"I let myself in. You should be more careful, my dear – the door was open. You will have every Old Age Pensioner in London invading your privacy if you do not lock it."

She had forgotten that Mr Gormann was coming to tea. He stood at the top of the staircase, fanning himself with a Panama hat.

"So! Every Old Age Pensioner in London *has* chosen to invade you."

It evidently did not occur to him that the three people dotted around her sitting-room had arrived unexpectedly, uninvited. The tone in which he spoke suggested reprimand, as if Evelyn should not spring social surprises on him, forcing him to meet people without his consent.

"You haven't met my parents," she said, quite flustered, not knowing whether the old man's arrival would make things easier – the conversation about Jeremy would surely now be brought to an end – or merely add tension to an already impossible situation. "Mr Gormann, Ma. And this is Mr Binding the vicar."

"I am enchanted." He had put on an unusually strong German accent, and had clearly decided to be as rude as possible. "To what do I owe this privilege?"

"Ma and Pa have called quite by surprise," said Evelyn, trying to exonerate herself.

"I read your autobiography with enjoyment, Sir Derek."

Evelyn's father twitched a little.

"Are you working on another book?"

"I'm glad you enjoyed it. I had hoped to publish a sequel, but for reasons best known to themselves, the publishers felt that the market was not yet ready for it."

"It's so nice to meet you, Mr Gormann," said Lady Tradescant. "We've heard so much about you."

"From Evelyn?"

"Naturally."

"How very touching that a daughter should speak to her mother about the Old Age Pensioner she happens to know. What, in particular, has she told you?"

Since Evelyn had never said anything to her mother about Mr Gormann, she wondered how Lady Tradescant would answer the old man's question.

"Oh, all about your wonderful work," she replied airily. "Derek has often talked about it, too. You know, I do believe we once met in the thirties. At one of those rather grand diplomatic dos. I'm not sure it wasn't at the Ribbentrops."

The remark could not have been less well judged.

Mr Gormann looked very angry and said, "You would not have recognised me. I was, perhaps, still wearing my monocle and carrying my whip."

"Perhaps you were." Her sunny expression suggested that she had entirely failed to sense the hostile tone of his remarks.

"People look so different with swastikas on their arms."

"Yes, I suppose they do."

"But actually, I am not altogether certain that I was not dining with the Führer that evening."

At first, a flash of recognition passed over Lady Tradescant's face, as if this piece of information confirmed her original suspicion that Mr Gormann had been an intimate of the Nazi leadership. Then her smile faded, as she realised that she was being mocked.

Sir Derek had risen to his feet. So had the clergyman. It was a tense moment: Evelyn wondered, for a second, whether her father were going to punch Mr Gormann on the nose. It was a horrible prospect: she felt that her wealth depended on it. Mr Gormann himself, almost purple with passion, stood resolutely clutching the handle of his walking-stick and staring into the diplomat's face. He, too, looked capable of laying about them all with his stick. Evelyn had heard about his bad temper from Pimlico Price, but had never seen it displayed before. It was dreadful.

The clergyman broke the silence.

"If I might put in a word," he began. Sir Derek interrupted him.

"We are going," he said, quietly.

"It seems to me that a very understandable misunderstanding . . ."

"We are going. Jean, collect your things together. We are not wanted here."

"I don't know what I said," whimpered Lady Tradescant.

"If we could only sit down and talk this one through . . ."

"Vicar, we are going."

"Ma, don't be upset."

"Goodbye, darling."

"Goodbye, Evelyn." Her father did not kiss her. "I had hoped that I could help, but there is clearly no point in staying."

"But don't be like this."

Mr Gormann stood, and said nothing, as the Tradescants and the clergyman shuffled down the stairs. Evelyn ran into the kitchen, where she could look down into the Mews below. She saw them walk hurriedly up towards Prince's Gate. None of them were talking, as far as could be made out.

"Was I very naughty?" Mr Gormann asked, boyish glee on his face as she came back towards him.

She threw her arms round his neck, squeezed him and sniffed.

"Naughty?"

"Your poor mother. But I do so very much dislike it when persons assume one to have been lucky to have escaped the Nuremberg trials."

"You saved the day."

"Dear child, in what way?"

Jeremy opened the bedroom door, his face green and sweaty.

"I say, sis, I'm afraid I've been sick on your counterpane."

9

Mr Gormann had not appeared to be disconcerted by the emergence of Jeremy on to that already confused scene. He took the boy's presence, if his bearing was anything to judge by, as unsurprising in the circumstances, one more or less member of the Tradescant family being unable to disrupt the tranquillity of his afternoon more than the tactlessness of their mother. He had never asked, since, why they had all congregated in Evelyn's flat, and he had shown no curiosity about the hostilities which were evidently in progress when he let himself in. It seemed, Evelyn thought, to fit in with the old man's contention that family life is frequently impossible, and where possible, to be avoided. "Families are *bad* for people – a long life at least teaches one something," was all that he had said. He did not appear to recollect any former conversations with Jeremy, asking to be reminded of the date and place of their encounters. Evelyn did not know whether this display of uncertainty was meant to spare her, or whether it was genuine. No chance was given her to make sure.

She saw Jeremy off a few days later at Victoria, laden with rucksacks. He introduced her to Gordon on the platform, but there was not much time to form any distinct impression. He was a dark young man, with glasses, difficult, unless prejudice blinded her, to imagine as the object of the kind of passion which had evidently been aroused in Jeremy. Apart from anything else, he had rather bad breath. She felt glad not to be hitch-hiking across Europe with him, mildly resentful that Jeremy should prefer the idea of doing so to staying a little longer in London with her.

Jeremy, and Pimlico Price, both away, Evelyn was thrown back increasingly on the company of Mr Gormann in the latter weeks of September. It was crisp, autumn weather of the most perfect kind, and they resumed their habit of walking in the afternoons.

An item that had been attracting a certain amount of attention in the news lately had been the acquisition by the National Gallery of a painting by Veronese. Some voices had been raised against the purchase of this apparently very pedestrian piece of work for what sounded a quite inordinately large sum of money. Trade figures, and the numbers of the unemployed, were thought to have been insufficiently considered. Mr Gormann felt strongly, in principle, that expenditure on works of art was "a Good Thing", and he could not see that the unemployed would be assisted in any way if the National Gallery did not buy the painting.

"But how can we tell unless we *see* this controversial thing?"

"We could go this afternoon, if you like. It's time I had a change from parks."

Evelyn had not been inside a picture-gallery since Geoffrey had gone to America. The impulse seemed a good one. They agreed to meet in Trafalgar Square, and put down their telephones.

It was one of those magnificently bright days that come when the summer is, properly speaking, over. The stone of St Martin's-in-the-Fields, the lions, the National Gallery itself, all recently cleaned, seemed to shine. Nelson was lost in a haze of light. In the distance, Pugin's Parliament buildings were traced delicately in the mist like an enchanted castle: weather to make one exuberantly happy, but also, in an idiotic way, *proud* to be in London. Evelyn felt a distinct swelling of emotion as she leaned over the balustrade at the entrance to the gallery, waiting for Mr Gormann to arrive.

The enormous cost of the painting they were about to see naturally increased her fascination at the prospect, money being greatly on her mind at the moment, and partly accounting for her feelings of wellbeing. Details of Mr Gormann's proposal to make her a beneficiary of his will had been discussed at greater length since his original allusion to the matter some weeks before. Contrary to what he had at first feared, he had managed to arrange things with his lawyer without consulting Pimlico. There would be no getting round telling him eventually, but for the present, Mr Gormann appeased his conscience by clinging to the fact that it was not all settled yet. Evelyn took this to mean that the will was not yet signed, not yet a legal document; but it was hard to extract any more information from Mr Gormann. About specific sums, he had been unforthcoming, but six figures had been mentioned.

Immeasurable calm had descended upon her, and she felt very close to him in a way that she had not done before.

Crowds milled past her into the gallery, talking a variety of languages, as Mr Gormann emerged from a taxi on the pavement below her.

The crispness of the air had brought him out in a greatcoat, trimmed with astrakhan at the collar.

He puffed up the steps to meet her and kissed her on the cheek. "I'm surprised you aren't in there seeing Dodo," he said breathlessly.

"Dodo?"

"David."

"Yes. But why?"

"Because he works here. Did you not know? We must look him up when we've seen the great work. I have been reading an article about it in one of the more intelligent weeklies. It's apparently a matter of some dispute what the painting is *of*."

Mr Gormann did not mean to imply, as Evelyn realised, that the work was of such inexact execution as to make figures, backgrounds, objects within it difficult to visualise, but rather that it was difficult of interpretation. Apparently in the manner of other allegorical paintings by Veronese in the National Gallery – hence

143

the strong motives for its purchase – it represented a feature of Love. Experts thought that it was probably meant to be part of a series, four of which were already identified. It had been called, tentatively, *Danger*, that word being used in the technical sense of courtly love-language, meaning that which discouraged the Lady from a true appreciation of her suitor. Others had attacked the title as anachronistic, pointing out that it was only an acceptable term in mediaeval usage, and had passed out of currency in Renaissance times. Something of a puzzle to art historians, the painting had been for a long time in private ownership, unknown as a Veronese. Only its striking resemblance to Veronese's *Scorn*, already in the National Gallery, had alerted the eye of an expert in the salerooms some years earlier.

Evelyn took Mr Gormann's arm when they were inside the building, as they walked up the superb staircase.

"Are you familiar with it all?" he asked her.

"I came here a lot in my first year in London."

"It is the finest gallery in the world. There is a perfect example of everything, and nowhere are paintings better hung."

"The Veronese looks as if it is off there to the left."

Hordes were milling in and out of a small room at the top of the staircase set aside for special exhibitions.

"We could look at the other Veroneses before we go in," said Mr Gormann. "He is a much underrated painter in our day – though not, of course, in his own."

The four works which *Danger* was said to resemble hung facing one another from the corners of the Venetian Room. The rough idea of the paintings, as Mr Gormann explained, was that each character in a given scene was enacting the quality represented, with the connivance of Cupid. In *Restraint*, for example, Cupid held the Lover back from the Lady, while she restrainedly veiled herself with drapery. In *Scorn*, Cupid trod on the stomach of the recumbent man while his mistress looked contemptuously away. Large and flamboyant, the paintings were not to Evelyn's taste, though she could see they were splendid enough.

"Let's look at *Danger* now," he said, his somewhat expansive account of the four paintings coming to an end.

On their way back through the Italian rooms, Evelyn paused by *The Baptism of Christ* by Piero della Francesca, a representation of which Jeremy had sent her on a postcard earlier in the summer. The figure in the background removing his shirt vividly brought to mind her own gesture of pulling off her pyjama top on Jeremy's camp bed, when he had followed the postcard to the flat that weekend. The incongruity of the association brought a perverse pleasure, distinct from her fondness for the painting itself. But the way that Piero's characters seemed so still, while not being lifeless, emphasised the importance of her first intimacy with Jeremy, her own action having been similarly "frozen", as an obvious turning-point in her fortunes. For one thing, the discovery that Jeremy simply satisfied her in the way that no lover had ever done before, released her from the position of weakness in which her earlier frustration inevitably placed her. In so far as she looked for sex with other people now, it was for purposes other than gratification, and this brought a sense of power. But also, on a more particular note, the fact that she had found this gratification with Jeremy, even if it were not to be repeated, gave her the trump card, should one now be needed, over Pimlico.

Danger, when they reached it, turned out to be not without relevance to her situation. Mounted on its own in a room otherwise empty of pictures, people milled round to stare at it, while a canned explanation of its features was relayed through a discreet loudspeaker. Evelyn held Mr Gormann's hand as they looked at it.

A large, white fleshy woman reclined on a bed which was exotically draped with silks, a coy hand held up toying with a nipple. Cupid lay with her, holding a protective hand on her stomach, and whispering in her ear while he held back with his other hand a Herculean man who leant over the woman. Another figure, plump but sexually indeterminate, peered from behind a grey Corinthian pillar, smooth as plasticine. A matronly figure, presumably Danger herself, spoke to the recumbent lady too, evidently urging her not to accept the man's advances. They all stood out crisply against a great expanse of bright blue sky. An olive branch blossomed behind the pillar. It was an accomplished piece, evidently in the manner of the other Veroneses which they had just seen.

The figure on the bed, if seen as herself, must have been being pursued by Pimlico Price; Mr Gormann, not an unbelievable transition, being cast in the role of the matronly Danger, magnificent in Venetian silks. Jeremy must clearly be Cupid, sharing her bed, and restraining the eager Pimlico from assaulting his sister. But the irony of the painting, as the canned lecture suggested, was to be found in the figure behind the pillar. What was his – if he were masculine – function? Clearly to restrain the Herculean man with his own counsels of caution. Then, one saw, the emphasis of the painting was entirely reversed. The man himself appeared as the dominant figure, prudently resisting the allurements of the woman, who, with the assistance of Cupid, attempted to ensnare him. Here, the position of the matronly bystander seemed hard to ascertain.

"This delicate, and yet crude, utterly Venetian conceit can be seen in the way that the painter has handled the olive leaves. There is a cavalier exuberance about it which has all the energy of Ariosto, all the pathos of a tune by Dowland."

The loudspeaker continued to emit bland noises of this kind in Third Programme tones.

"I dislike intensely this pseudo art-history," said Mr Gormann loudly.

"Ssh," said a woman in a scarlet overcoat.

"Go and search out Dodo. He will give us a coherent account of the matter."

From what little she had seen of Dodo de Waal, coherence was not something which Evelyn would have expected of him. But, having extracted directions from Mr Gormann about where to find his office, she set off, leaving the old man sandwiched in an enormous crowd contemplating the tableau arranged on the wall.

"We shall probably find it is a Platonist debate between Body and Soul," he grunted, as if that were an equally ludicrous subject for a painting.

Dodo de Waal, inseparable in Evelyn's mind from Dicky Evans, with whom he swam from time to time in the pool at Fish Square, worked in water-colours. It came back to her now. After a short spell at one of the Bond Street galleries he had been lucky and found his present post at the National Gallery, which was much more to her taste. On the few occasions when she had bumped into him, he had always seemed pleasant enough, if embarrassingly affected. He and Dicky Evans had never been properly explained to her. No one had told her how they came to know Mr Gormann; and, entirely illogically, she felt entitled to this information. It was this which accounted for a certain reserve in her manner towards them, despite the fact that she knew her feelings in the matter to be unjustifiable, and she would have been affronted had anyone demanded of her a *reason* why she belonged to Mr Gormann's *entourage*. She felt that she *belonged* and this required no justification. On a simpler level, she was a friend. Dodo de Waal and Dicky Evans could probably make similar, if not stronger, claims. Certainly they were friends of longer standing than she.

She found Dodo drinking coffee with a girl who looked like a secretary.

"How *nice*," he said, fluttering his eye-lashes, and making the adjective have about three syllables. Pimlico always said that Dodo would have been best employed on the stage, with his innate genius for making the most innocent utterances smack of sexual *double-entendre*.

"Mr Gormann and I have come to see the Veronese."

"But *of course*. This is Elizabeth." He indicated the secretary as though she were a pet animal. "And this is Monica."

"Evelyn, actually."

He hung his tongue out shamefacedly and looked at the ceiling. "*Sorry*. How *awful*."

"That's all right."

"We were just having a little of what one might call coffee."

"Might call?"

"If one were in a totally frivolous mood. Which I am. Care to join us?"

"Mr Gormann was wondering if you could come and explain the painting to us. He seems to think the explanation coming over the loudspeaker isn't much cop."

"So like Theo. I must tell Ray. He'll *die*. Thinks of it as his *chef-d'oeuvre*, as one might say. Do you know Theo?" he asked, turning to the secretary, "Theo Gormann?"

The secretary wore a blank, slightly bored look which suggested that she knew no one.

"Well, I had better come I suppose. Though Theo must know more about Veronese than I do. I haven't really *done* Veronese, as it were, since I was at the Courtauld Institute."

"I thought you were an expert."

"English water-colours, dear. But I dare say that I could turn what I laughingly call my mind to something else as a special favour. I haven't had much to do with the arrival of the Veronese."

"It cost rather a lot, didn't it?"

"A positively wicked amount! It's the only thing to be said in its favour as far as I can see. Still, what can one do when peers of the realm go bankrupt? It was the Earl of Rickmansworth's, you know. It's all supposed to be a deadly secret, but of course it's common knowledge."

"The difficulty seems to be the figure behind the column," said Evelyn, who had really thought the explanation given over the loudspeaker quite good.

"Indeed, yes," Dodo agreed. "Between ourselves, I suspect that it's all the tiniest bit naughty."

"How are you liking your job here?" she asked after they had sipped their coffee in silence for a minute or two.

"Of course, you could hardly call it a job," he corrected her. "Would you call it a job, Elizabeth?"

The secretary took no notice.

"Good heavens, what's that?"

Evelyn felt the floor quiver beneath her feet before she heard any noise. It was a deep, shatteringly loud boom, so powerful that it shook her whole body. Dodo's face became suddenly serious. She noticed a sort of dignity about his appearance which had not been apparent before. She felt unaccountably frightened. Something serious had happened. The secretary had put down her coffee-cup and was looking for guidance to Dodo.

"We'd better get out," he said.

It still did not occur to Evelyn what had happened. Dodo had taken her arm, and the secretary's, and was hurrying them out of the office.

The gallery was empty, but there was a strong smell of smoke, and a noisy, distant echo of human voices as they rushed down some stairs.

The French rooms were full of smoke, drifting towards them. One saw the blue haze of Claudes and Corots behind a smoky film rushing past.

"Bloody Irish," Dodo was saying, "it was bound to happen sooner or later."

Violent fear, anger, anxiety for Mr Gormann overcame her, a cluster of intense emotions that made her stiffen as she became aware that a bomb had exploded. As they scurried through the empty gallery, the sound of screaming, becoming louder and louder, echoed in their ears.

"Stop!"

There was a policeman just ahead of them.

"What are you doing here?" he demanded.

"Get these women out of here." Dodo handed Evelyn and the secretary over. There was a sort of heroism about his failure to answer the question.

"Was there anyone else in your part of the building, sir?" The policeman evidently recognised Dodo as a man in authority.

"Not so far as I know."

"Come this way. There's no need to panic. This way. You too, please, sir."

They ran past the English landscapes, Stuart portraits, out to the top of the staircase where, only a short while before, Evelyn had stood with Mr Gormann. Flames and smoke poured out of the room where the Veronese was, or had been. Men in uniform — ambulance drivers, firemen, milled round. Horrible cries came through the smoke. People were being carried off on stretchers.

"Are there still people in there?"

She was horrified, amazed.

"This way, miss, please."

"Come on, Evelyn."

"Let me go."

A stretcher passed them and she saw that its ghastly load was Mr Gormann.

"Let me go, let me past, he's mine, he's mine."

She wriggled free, leaving Dodo and the policeman at the top of the staircase, and ran after the stretcher-bearers.

"He's mine . . . He's mine." She was shouting it now.

The circular doors had been removed; blasted? She ran through.

"You must let me see him," she gasped to the ambulance man.

"You had better come along with us," he said.

There were policemen holding back the crowds, uniformed officials everywhere, preventing people from running about. It was miraculous that she got through. No consciousness of what was happening — of a detailed kind, anyway — came to her. She only felt an overwhelming desire to be near the old man.

Somebody took her arm and helped her into the ambulance. It moved off at great speed before she had a chance to sit down.

Mr Gormann was covered with a blanket, only his face visible. His eyes were closed. His lips seemed to be wreathed in a smile, but, after a short time, his face became contorted with pain.

An ambulance man held her hand and told her not to watch. She shut her eyes until they reached the hospital.

After that, she sat on a green, plastic-covered chair in a bare white room and watched the minutes glide slowly past on an electric clock affixed to the wall.

Somebody came and offered her tea, which she refused. There was a poster on the opposite wall about the dangers of lung cancer. She lit a cigarette.

A little later, someone came and sat beside her, holding a clipboard stuffed with paper.

"You were with the old gentleman?"

"Yes."

"Well, he's in the theatre now. I'm afraid they've had to do an emergency operation."

"Does that mean . . .?"

"We'd just like to take down a few particulars." Kindly, but inexorably, the voice insisted.

Evelyn gave her own name and address and telephone number as next of kin. She was asked Mr Gormann's age, address and religion. She did not know his age.

It was funny how little she knew about him, really. She felt lost in overwhelming regret; that their friendship had been so short; that they had chosen to see this controversial painting in the first place. She felt sure, without the kind voices of the people in the hospital to warn her, that he was going to die. The randomness of it appalled her. Not until a considerable while afterwards did she even begin to think of the *people* who had planted the bomb in the gallery. She merely thought of death, violent death at that, as an adversary itself, awaiting its occurrence with agitation as a thing of which she had no experience.

After a long period of just sitting, she went to the telephones and tried to ring up Pimlico. She had forgotten that he was in Scotland. She felt terribly in need of talking to someone; also, with great panic, a sense of there being things that she ought to have been doing. For all Mr Gormann's large circle, there was nobody there. Nobody was to know what had happened. Still with 2p in her hand and not knowing what to do next, she dialled the school's telephone number. The principal, Miss Wing, was remarkably understanding; Evelyn felt soothed by her voice. After their short conversation, she felt comforted by the thought that at least one of the "things" to be done was done. She was not to return to work until she felt able to.

When she returned to the waiting-room, it was full of people. Families were there, children misbehaving. Reporters from the newspapers were asking people for their reactions to the explosion.

"What will you feel if your husband dies?"

"Have you any message for the terrorists?"

"Have you seen your son?"

She escaped, just in time, into the corridor. For the first time that day, she felt deeply frightened. The bomb, in the event, had caused too much confusion to induce fear of the kind that overwhelmed her now. She had been too anxious to find Mr Gormann, too shocked by the fact that he was being carried on a stretcher, to feel much terror for herself. But the prospect of facing the interrogations of the callous, vulgar little men whose business was to make a "story" of the episode was chilling, and frightful. Above all, which was absurd, she dreaded having to explain to them who she was, and how she came to be attached to Mr Gormann.

She went to the lavatory. There were women there, crying. When she came out, she paced up and down the hospital corridors. Perhaps what was most alarming was how alone she felt. She wished that Dodo had come with her in the ambulance. She grew gradually aware of how much of herself she had lost to Mr Gormann. The only man who could have helped her through this nightmare was Gormann himself; no one else. Her separation from him was unbearable, her need for him never more strongly felt. Life had presented its minor share of upsets to her, but things had always been all right in the end, hitherto. She had almost come to develop the favoured sense that, whatever happened, she would land on her feet. Now, no such confidence seemed fitting. For the first time, there would be no evading the hurt.

It seemed a very long time before the doctors came to see her.

They seemed alarmingly young; her age or less. They told her that Mr Gormann had been taken into Intensive Care. His condition was critical. Surgeons were doing all that they could. The young men were whiskery in an unattractive way. Their youth disgusted her, and they smelt vilely of TCP.

If she left a telephone number, the hospital would call her when the operation was complete. There was nothing, at the time, that could be gained by her waiting there.

She clambered into her flat in a daze. She had no idea what time it was and was amazed to find, on consulting her alarm-clock, that only two hours had passed.

Her ability to *wait* had never been tested before. She found that she did not possess it.

She was unable to sit down, unable to be still. She went into the bathroom, and scrupulously tidied away stray bras and jerseys which were draped over chairs. She then went to her bedroom. She stripped the bed and remade it thoroughly, smoothing out the bottom sheet and carefully tucking in the blankets with hospital corners.

She emerged, went to the broom cupboard and decided to vacuum clean the whole flat.

It was while she was doing this that the telephone rang.

"Hullo."

Just a bleeping sound came at the other end.

"Hullo. Hullo."

"Evelyn?" It was Pimlico's voice.

"Oh, God! John, it's Evelyn. Listen. Mr Gormann is in hospital."

"Hullo. Hullo? Evelyn? I'm in a call box. It's difficult with my mother . . ."

"John!" She shouted the name. A slow bleeping interrupted them. She burst into tears.

Almost at once, the telephone rang again.

"John?"

"This is the Westminster Hospital. Is that Miss Tradescant?"

"Yes." She spoke so quietly, that the voice at the other end made her repeat it.

"Mr Gormann has been taken out of Intensive Care. He seems to be fairly comfortable."

"And can I see him?"

"He has been moved to Hampshire Ward. The Sister will tell you how to find him. Visiting time stops officially at half past eight, but I expect that they will waive the rule a little in this case."

"Thank you . . . thank you."

"If there is anything else that you want to know, you can find out at the hospital."

It was a kind voice, professionally trained to talk to people in her position. It calmed her, and she thought with quiet, though intellectual, horror of the fact that all over London were people waiting by telephones to know if other people were dead or alive.

She did not know what time it was.

She caught a taxi to the hospital.

Warm evening sunshine shone indifferently down on scenes often frequented with Mr Gormann. The thought of him as a real person, rather than as an object of panic, now came back to her. He would have broken bones. She should have asked about it on the telephone; she thought of slow walks that she would take with him, his legs in plaster. It would be she who pottered about the flat in Fish Square and made the tea. She wondered, almost with amusement, whether he would require a bath chair.

At the hospital, everyone was kind. She walked down a corridor which was painted a very pale shade of green. Visitors, of whom there were a fair number at that time of evening, looked strangely incongruous in outside clothes. The occasional patient was wheeled along on a trolley. She passed the doors of wards, and saw, briefly through plastic windows, little groups huddled about the ends of beds; squat bedside cabinets laden with flowers and cards; jaunty, unhappy old men in dressing-gowns.

She followed signs saying "Hampshire Ward". When she got

there, a Negress asked her whom she wanted to see. When she told her, the black nurse went away and came back with a white nurse.

"Mr Gormann is asleep," she said. "But you can see him, if you like."

She led Evelyn through the ward, which was evidently set aside for geriatric nursing. To right and left, people lay in various states of mutilation. Some had their legs in pulleys aloft in the air. Some were sitting bolt upright in frames. Some of them looked too old to be alive, with no teeth and little scrubs of hair, and large, vacant hollows around their eyes. It was not always easy to tell whether they were men or women.

"He is in the room at the end." The sister spoke in a quiet, comforting voice.

Evelyn pushed open the door.

They should have warned her.

Her imagination had not dwelt on what the explosion would have done to an aged human body. At first, she thought that she was going to faint. And then, she found she was crying. It was unrecognisable as Mr Gormann.

His right leg was suspended in a pulley like the ones she had passed in the ward. It was coated with plaster, but blood was seeping through the plaster, making it hideous, the first thing that met the eye when opening the door. The top of one arm was in plaster; so was a shoulder. The rest of the body was barely covered by a loose sheet. It was quite naked. Hardly a patch of it was the colour of flesh. Deep purple and black marks disfigured the whole of it.

Mercifully, the face had been spared. But they had put a thin plastic tube up one nostril, and a plastic oxygen mask veiled the mouth and chin. It hardly seemed like a human body at all; more like a ghastly machine of which some of the necessary components were wounded limbs. It sprawled terribly. It was much wider than a body would normally be, lying on a bed. And the arms and legs stuck out at extraordinary angles. Everywhere, cranes, tubes, bottles, bags, drips added to the air of unreality. Something from a bottle was being dripped into his nose; something from another bottle into his arm; and a polythene bag full of urine flopped down beneath the folds of the sheet.

What was worst, this hideous conglomeration of blood and plaster was clearly and vigorously alive. The noise of his breathing was terrible, like amplified snoring, only much less even in timing.

She squeezed her way past all the equipment and kissed the old man on the forehead. It was a good thing to do. It at once dispelled her fears.

She stood there for a long time, holding the tips of his fingers gently and occasionally murmuring his name, that she had only used once in his presence before. As time passed, she ceased altogether to be disgusted. A feeling that in more guarded moments she would have unquestionably dismissed as soupy was welling up inside her. She felt proud. Not proud of herself, or proud of Mr Gormann, but simply proud that life fought against its elimination with such pathetic vehemence.

She wondered how long it would all go on. Sometimes, the breathing appeared to stop and Evelyn's own heart missed a beat. Then, after an unconscionable time, the body let out an undignified snort and resumed its breathing again.

The longer she stayed, the more she was caught up in the impressive drama of this object's struggle to remain alive. Every breath seemed to be an adventure, a triumph.

The black nurse came in after an interval and began to rearrange the equipment. She peered at the bottle from which the drip was coming and then removed it.

She came back with a full bottle and fixed it to the drip with metal clamps.

Evelyn watched her tensely. It seemed impossible that this was not giving Mr Gormann pain. But he did not appear to be reacting at all.

"Sister would like a word with you on your way out," said the black nurse, with a kind smile.

Evelyn felt afraid to leave Mr Gormann now. But she did leave quite shortly afterwards. The sister told her that there was a fear that he had broken his spine and might never walk again. She promised to ring up Evelyn in her flat if there were any "developments" during the night.

Evelyn surprised herself that night by sleeping for thirteen hours. After breakfast, the telephone rang. It was Pimlico.

She tried to tell him the news gently, but he had guessed most of it from accounts of the explosion in the newspapers.

"Where are you now?"

"I'm in Glasgow. I'm catching a plane at midday. There isn't an earlier one. I'll meet you at the hospital."

"All right."

"There's not really any hope, is there, Evelyn?"

"No," she said quietly, "I don't suppose that there is."

But rest and sleep had encouraged her. She had begun to feel in her bones, as her mother would have said, that Mr Gormann was going to live. She telephoned the hospital and they said he was "comfortable". She assumed that this meant that he was alive and not actually writhing in pain.

When she arrived there again about an hour later, he looked just as he had done the night before. She stayed about an hour, during which a nurse brought her a cup of very milky coffee. At about half past eleven, a very tall, bespectacled man of about thirty put his head round the door. At first, she thought he was one of the doctors.

"Richard Evans," he said politely, stretching across the apparatus to shake her by the hand. "You must be Evelyn Tradescant."

"Yes. Yes, I am."

"Ghastly, isn't it?"

She agreed.

"Much better not to live through it," he said, averting his gaze from Mr Gormann. His hands quivered. Evelyn felt sorry for him.

"Felt I must come," he murmured. "Theo has been such a pet to me."

"Mm."

"My mother was in a coma for a fortnight," he continued. "They can go on for an interminable period, you know."

"How's Dodo?" she asked.

"They let him home last night. Only slight burns, so he was lucky."

"Burns?"

"Yes. After you'd left him, he went back and helped people carry the injured down to ambulances. I'm awfully cross with him, needless to say."

Richard Evans looked as if he was incapable of being cross with anyone.

"I . . . I didn't know. Send him my love," said Evelyn.

"I shall. He was up at Magdalen with your brother I gather?"

"Just for a year, they overlapped."

A terrible snort from the bed interrupted the conversation which had been conducted in the most subdued tones over by the door.

"Well, I dare say that we shall be meeting again," said Richard Evans. He disappeared.

Other visitors came in the course of the morning. Evelyn stayed, feeling almost protective of the old man. Some middle-aged women of about fifty came in and did not appear to notice her. They stroked his forehead and called him Theo and made the sign of the cross.

After lunch, she came and found a priest sitting in the room with Pimlico Price. Pimlico was weeping copiously and uncontrollably. Evelyn had never seen him in this condition, and, as on so many occasions with him, she felt embarrassed. The little clergyman sat impassively by Pimlico's side, looking as if it were all in a day's work and very much the kind of thing he was used to. But his face was not without compassion.

Pimlico did not look up when she came into the room. He just sat there crying. The clergyman quietly said, "Good morning," to her.

"I have given Mr Gormann the last rites of the church," he

remarked. "He seems very peaceful."

"Thank you very much," said Evelyn. She did not know what he meant, but he evidently intended to be kind.

She put an arm round Pimlico's shoulder, not in any endeavour to comfort him – she knew that would be pointless – but simply to impress upon him the fact that she was there.

"It's worse than you said," he moaned.

"Yes."

"It's terrible."

"Yes."

"Poor Theo."

At that moment, the nurse came in to inform them that the doctors wanted to examine Mr Gormann. Evelyn said that they would go out for half an hour.

They walked along the Embankment in silence. Pimlico accepted a cigarette from her. She was smoking too much.

"Tell me again what happened," he said. "Exactly what happened."

She recounted as much as she could remember of the explosion. He asked a lot of questions to which she knew no answer.

They went into a pub and drank gin and tonic. Neither of them felt hungry, but they shared a cheese sandwich.

"And do they know how long?"

"If they do, they haven't said," she said.

She had not reckoned on how long it would all take. She and Pimlico went back to the hospital after lunch and sat with Mr Gormann until about six. Then they went out to supper together. After supper, they agreed that Pimlico should spend the evening by the bedside and ring her if there were any "developments". They found themselves talking in hospital jargon. She would spend the morning there and ring Pimlico at his office. He was in the middle of a business crisis which even this disaster could not be allowed to interrupt. She was glad to be separated from him for a while. She had not prepared herself for Pimlico's reaction, and she found it emotionally tiring.

The watching continued for several days. It was as if there had never been any other kind of existence. Her arrivals at the bedside and her vigils there acquired the quality of habit and routine almost immediately. The ghastly honking noise which the breathing made through the oxygen mask was as easy to get used to as the sound of a human voice. She became hardly aware of what was happening.

On Saturday evening, she and Pimlico watched together. The nurse said that there were signs of Mr Gormann's rallying. There was even talk of his recovering consciousness. This worried them both, for it was impossible to imagine him conscious in his present state without terrible pain. Evelyn had grown used to him as someone who was unconscious.

The breathing gurgled irregularly on.

At about ten, they decided to go home. Pimlico hailed a taxi outside the hospital and dropped her off at Prince's Gate Mews. He patted her gently on the bottom as they parted.

There was still a little milk left in the fridge. She decided to make herself some Horlicks and to read a Beetle book before going to sleep.

She sipped the foaming hot drink and peered at the photographs of mint leaves devoured by the larva of Tortoise Beetles.

She wondered why she had allowed herself, when still a schoolgirl, to have been pushed into reading Mathematics at Cambridge. There was everything to be said for Biology.

10

Cold wind blew in across the Channel. The sea was grey and choppy. Lights on the Palace Pier stretched out into the dusk. She had strolled there in the morning – almost the only person around – and she had bought a fresh doughnut. Cars roared along the promenade: rush hour was starting early. A few boys loitered on the shingle by the water's edge, kicking stones from time to time, or throwing empty bottles against the girders of the pier. The man selling balloons was not in his usual place today: no trade. The aquarium was shut. She looked out of the window at the waves and wondered if it was time to rouse Mr Gormann from his nap.

To Evelyn, the explosion, and life before it happened, though not much over two months ago, seemed almost immeasurably remote, the passing of the holiday season and, gradually, the complete emptying of the place contributing to the illusion that time, if it was not actually standing still, had begun to move at a different pace. London felt very far away.

As soon as it had become apparent that Mr Gormann was going to pull through, Pimlico Price had returned to Scotland, events there demanding his full attention. The firm was still without a managing director, and, until a more acceptable arrangement could be found, he was obliged to stay there himself.

He had not been pressing about the proposal he had made to her, months ago, in the Bunch of Grapes. Apart from the obvious awkwardness of the situation, there had been too much to worry about in the hospital for much talk of the future to seem possible. They had been very affectionate with one another, and, during their meals together, they had sometimes held hands under the table while he talked to her about the crisis at the "Chewy" factory. Their conversations had not been in the least interesting, but she felt soothed to have a companion with whom she could share the hospital visiting.

When Lady Tradescant read about the explosion in the *Daily Telegraph*, she wrote to Evelyn at once, offering to help. Kindness came so naturally to her that you could not even wonder at her magnanimity. But, although her mother's offer pleased her greatly, Evelyn wrote back to say that she would rather be alone.

There had been no word from Sir Derek. One would not have expected it. Even though it was his wife's tactlessness which had brought their meeting with Mr Gormann to such a ludicrous conclusion, it was he who had been made to look foolish. Whatever *coup* he had attempted to bring off by his mission to her flat, it clearly could not have been less successful. Even she, whose nerves had become so very hard of late, would find the reconciliation with her father difficult, when it eventually came. But it was hard to see how Jeremy could be persuaded to face his father for a very long time, even if he were nearer home. The last that she had heard was a postcard from Turkey, some three weeks ago, announcing his intention to winter there. Gordon had left him almost as soon as they reached Calais, but since the postcard spoke in the first person plural, she assumed that fresh companionship had been acquired *en route*. She missed the boy desperately, felt anxious about him. Jeremy in Istanbul could be nothing but unsafe.

Mr Gormann had broken a leg and a collar-bone. Fears for a broken spine had been almost immediately dismissed, the chief cause for concern being not the fractures themselves, but the shock sustained by the heart. Once he came round, he made a rapid recovery and enjoyed being fussed over by the nurses. Pimlico's instinct to move him into a private nursing-home while the worst of his burns and bruises healed was quickly squashed. Evelyn remembering his fear of solitude – the assertion that suicide was the only intelligent activity when in solitary confinement came to mind – was unsurprised by Mr Gormann's unwillingness to find himself in a private ward.

He knew himself to be at his best when on display. As a "bomb victim", in the newspapers' phrase, he had achieved a good deal of welcome notoriety, gleefully making statements to any reporter who found his way into the ward at visiting-time. There had been nothing like it, from his point of view, since the high days of CND, it being his fate, as he whimsically observed, to be associated in the public mind with bombs; whether banning them, or being blown up by them made little odds.

BOMB VICTIM APPEALS TO TERRORISTS was a headline which much delighted him, the result of an interview with a reporter from one of the more vulgar Sunday papers. "'Next time try the Tate,' was bomb victim Baron Theo Gormann's plucky bid last night from his hospital bed, where he is recovering from last week's atrocity in the National Gallery in which two people were killed and fifteen injured . . .'"

"Was I very naughty?" he asked her. "Those time-wasting abstracts they have accumulated on Millbank always seemed to me particularly boring."

"The Royal Academy Summer Exhibition could do with blowing to bits just as much."

"I disagree with you, dear girl. Weekend painting should be encouraged. It keeps people off the roads, and away from their families. That at least contributes to human happiness."

Evelyn had once had a friend at Cambridge – it was Anna on her corridor, the one who smoked a pipe – whose constant contention about people of whom she mildly disapproved was that they needed a bomb putting under them. This violent solution to the apathy, neo-Toryism, Philistinism, uncharitability or heterosexuality of her friends had always struck Evelyn as extreme. She had now come to revise her opinion. Mr Gormann was distinctly more playful, less given to fits of melancholy, since the explosion. At first, she thought that it was because he enjoyed the publicity which his suffering had aroused, and the comparatively captive audience provided by his ward-mates. But his high spirits had persisted. When it was time for him to be discharged from hospital, the idea of a seaside hotel as a place of convalescence had been mooted, and it appeared to give him great pleasure. He had not even asked Evelyn if she would accompany him. She had assumed that she would do so. A large hotel on the sea front where he was accustomed to spend a few weeks each year anyway seemed the obvious place to choose. He was known there and he liked it. There would be no difficulty about meals in his rooms.

When Evelyn said what a pity it was that he had chosen to have his accident when the season was more or less over, he had disagreed with her strongly.

"Holiday towns are at their best when they are deserted. There is nothing more depressing than the sight of one's fellow mortals trying to enjoy themselves. Doctor Johnson never wrote anything truer than his observation that man is not born for happiness. Pleasure domes are invariably unhappy places. But, on the other hand – to parody another of Johnson's sayings – a man is seldom more innocently employed than when he is trying to enjoy himself. Seaside towns have a perpetually innocent, childish quality. I know that people think that this is rather a sinful town. They used to have a bell in this hotel to summon people back to their own bedrooms before early morning tea. But in my view, that is a fairly *innocent* sort of sin. People come here to spend their money, and not to make it. And that gives the place a refreshingly joyful quality."

So, there they had been for nearly two months. Evelyn had been out for walks on her own – Mr Gormann was not mobile yet – but most of her time had been spent with him. She saw now more clearly how much it suited him to have decided to

entrust so much of his wealth to a conscientious young woman,
willing to tend the sick. Sooner or later, without the bomb,
decrepitude would have set in, and the companionship of such a
person would have become desirable. Perhaps in some sense, she
had been purchased. She did not mind. She found him very
charming, and the sum to be provided was princely. They talked,
played chess, listened to the wireless, read aloud. Browning,
almost at the last minute shoved into a suitcase as they were leaving
Fish Square, had become a favourite. They enjoyed the muddle of
pagan and Christian sensuality in the Bishop's desire for a magnificent tomb in St Praxed's; and the outrageous impatience of the
Duke of Ferrara with his last Duchess. "Poor man, I know how he
felt. 'Who passed without much the same smile?' – one feels like
that in the presence of bar-maids and air-hostesses. To be married
to such a person would be intolerable." One which they found to
read aloud very well was "Two in the Campagna", with its haunting lines:

> Just when I seemed about to learn!
>   Where is the thread now? Off again!
> The old trick! Only I discern –
>   Infinite passion, and the pain
>   Of finite hearts that yearn.

Evelyn enjoyed Mr Gormann's fondness for Browning more than
she enjoyed the poetry itself. She found it jerky, opaque, difficult.
But these lines stayed in the mind on her solitry walks to the end of
the Palace Pier and back each morning. They seemed suitable to
her own position, the odd juxtaposition of infinite passion and
yearning with the word "trick". In a great many senses, she had
been tricked into joining Mr Gormann's circle, flattered and cajoled
into becoming his companion, probably for the rest of his life.
But she, too, had not been innocent of trickery. It was catching.
She felt sure that she would not have deceived her parents about
Jeremy if it had not been for her friendship with Mr Gormann.

More, not without some consciousness of what she was doing, she had come between Mr Gormann and Pimlico Price. The thing had not been wholly above board.

Mr Gormann, for instance, knew nothing of the possibility that she might marry Pimlico; and, if only in so far as she thought it would probably remove her from his immediate circle, the news could not fail to displease him. Pimlico and she had both seen the necessity of keeping him in the dark. There had been a good deal of trickery.

Love itself was a trick, as Browning perceived, played on oneself by others, and by oneself, and resulting – whatever its insincere beginnings – in "infinite passion" and pain. Sexual considerations played an unimportant part in her discovery, while he was still unconscious in the hospital, of how much she loved Mr Gormann. In his present battered state, there would have been little likelihood of love-making, even if it had been on the cards otherwise. But passion and pain could exist to a surprising intensity without sex, she found, just as sexual desire could exist, and be gratified, without the involvement of the passions. Sex itself played "tricks" when it made people believe otherwise. As she lay in bed at night, desires came to her, as it were out of the blue; memories of former lovers and the occasional ecstasy they had provided. If the opportunity of ecstasy presented itself, again, she knew that she would probably take it. But it would not detract from her "infinite passion" for Mr Gormann, which had involved her so absolutely, and, in so short a time, become the dominant feature of her life.

They had been days of quiet, deep happiness. She had stopped trying to solve the riddle of Mr Gormann's personality, and found, in the quietude of everyday conversation, that she had come to know him: his fears, his petulance, his gentleness, his erudition all manifesting themselves in numberless ways without specific conversational allusion to them.

It was almost dark – the sea only visible as light was reflected on its turbulent surface. She left her room and went next door to Mr Gormann.

He was propped against the pillows, writing letters.

"I've done three," he said. "Not bad for a bomb victim."

"You shouldn't tire yourself."

"Writing letters? That's not tiring."

"You were supposed to be sleeping."

"I want to make Patterson stir himself about this will. I have never had any illusions about my own mortality. Being a bomb victim brings it home, as you would say. You do realise, don't you, that if I had died in the National Gallery, you would be penniless — apart from the money we've put in your current account."

"Don't let's talk about money." She had feared as much. The thought sickened her. It was nightmarish. The spirit of detachment with which Mr Gormann was approaching the whole matter was presumably an indication of the "extraordinary astuteness" in financial dealings with which Pimlico had attributed him. It had the tone of a psychologist discussing sex, or a theologian God: an almost eerily cold ability to view cerebrally areas of life coloured with "infinite passion".

"We must talk about money a little, my dear. And then we can have tea. After tea, I want to play chess, so you must arrange the board on the table by the window."

"I'll do it now."

"But you must listen as you do so. I have written to Patterson telling him that you are to have a third of my estate when I die. I have also written to my bank" — he waved a second envelope — "telling them to transfer some more money to your account."

She turned to him as she arranged the pieces on the board. They were large and ivory, a favourite heirloom. She held the Red King in her hand.

"Aren't you going to ask me how much?"

"It doesn't interest me. No. I'm sorry, that sounds awfully ungrateful, and you know that that's the last thing I want to be. I mean . . ."

"Dear child, I know what you mean. I've put eighty in your deposit account." He never used the word "thousand" when discussing money. "You had better make up your mind to do something with it. It will be worth nothing by the end of the year."

"What about John?" she asked. Her fingers clutched the Red King nervously. The head of the piece was divided from the base by a slender neck, slightly cracked ever since she had first seen it. As she asked the question, she felt the piece break – just come apart in her hand, like the parlour-maid in a drawing-room farce.

"That's in my third letter," said the old man. "It's time he was told."

"But his factory . . ." She did not want to give away too much. Mr Gormann still knew nothing, as far as she was aware, of Pimlico's conversation with her at the Bunch of Grapes, although he must have been aware that Pimlico thought he was throwing his money away.

"When it comes to a choice, as everything does sooner or later, you mean more to me than John's sugar candy palace." He spoke a little breathlessly. "Do you think, my dear, that you could try to open a window? It has become insufferably hot in this room."

"Are you sure that you feel all right? It does not seem hot to me."

"Do as I say."

"We could easily ring up the doctor. They said that . . ."

"Open the window. I shall ring down for the tea. I shall be all right in a minute."

His face was darkening. He was plainly not "all right". She felt powerless. He was near the telephone, and speaking into it.

"Yes. And, if it were possible, cream horns. Yes. No, China tea. Thank you." He put the receiver down.

> "O that 'twere possible
> After long grief and pain
> To find a place that did quite well
> Tea and cream horns again."

The formulaic banter had been automatically assumed to disguise obvious bodily discomfort. The colour of his face was dreadful.

"Before I have my tea, I must hobble in there," he said, indicating the bathroom. "All right in a minute. Have you ever known a bomb victim after cream horns?"

He propelled himself with extreme difficulty from the bed to the bathroom, and refused Evelyn's offer of help. It was terrifying to see his face threatening to resume the appalling contortions which it had worn in hospital.

"Go back to arranging the board," he said crossly when she tried to take an arm. "There's that King you're holding. It's very fragile. Don't clutch it too hard."

The crutches looked as if they were biting into his shoulder. When he at last lurched into the bathroom — he seemed to take about an hour getting there, though it couldn't have been more than a few minutes — she put the broken Red King down on the chess board. Aware that she was quite incompetent to deal with the situation, she debated whether to run out and fetch a doctor, deciding against it on the grounds that Mr Gormann should not be left alone. The waitress who brought up the tea could be dispatched to fetch medical help.

When he came out of the bathroom, he had regained a normal colour and seemed less breathless. Tea came, and he drank a cup, but he did not have a cream horn; nor anything else to eat that day. When Evelyn confessed to having broken the Red King, he seemed strangely uninterested. They played, after tea, but his mind was not on the game. His eyes had a distant, thoughtful look, as if they knew the significance of his sudden "turn". It was as if the face of a pursuer, becoming increasingly familiar, now close behind, had been glimpsed in a mirror.

The slightness of the episode — particularly when compared with the cataclysmic noise, and smell and horror of the bomb explosion — was so extreme as to make Evelyn feel that she was being over-anxious. He had just felt hot, and gone to the lavatory. But they had been almost shy with each other at tea. Both knew what was in the other's mind, but neither dared to mention it. To have been delivered from so final a separation, and so recently, had filled them both, perhaps, with too much optimism for the future. They decided to have early nights. Mr Gormann said he would promise to see the doctor in the morning. He was, he said, having difficulty in passing water. Evelyn left his room at about eight, having read him some Browning. She went downstairs and sat in the Television Lounge, but the coloured images flickering on the screen failed to distract her. The last phase had been entered.

She had known him barely six months, she recollected, lying awake through the night, able, when traffic subsided, to hear the sea beyond her bedroom window. She tried to piece together the story of their friendship, and found it impossible. In some ways, she had known the whole thing would happen the moment she encountered him in Kensington Gardens: like every important thing in life, it seemed inevitable. But *how* they came to know each other, and love each other; by what degrees their intimacy had deepened, or unfolded – she was unsure which metaphor was the more apt – she found it hard to remember. The strands were too complex and delicate to be seen as it were with the naked eye of memory.

Not much inclined to view life as if it were a kind of moral obstacle race designed to improve us, she could not say whether knowing Mr Gormann had made her better. But it had changed her: she could perceive that easily enough by finding it impossible to imagine herself behaving, speaking, thinking now as she had done at the beginning of the year. Even this was difficult to analyse. She had merely found, when meeting friends of longer standing, that they were expecting her to be a person that had mysteriously ceased to exist. They were out of touch. She had gone on, leaving former characters of her own behind her like old clothes. As thoughts about death had come to preoccupy her, she had been haunted by the lines of a hymn they had sung every Remembrance Sunday at her school –

Time like an ever-rolling stream
Bears all its sons away . . .

It seemed as perfect an expression as any of the fact of our mortality. But as she thought about it now, she saw that it was Time, not Death, which changed us.

> They fly forgotten, as a dream
> Dies at the opening day.

It was as true of friends with whom she had lost contact, former lovers, old colleagues – all, presumably, pursuing their lives without her, as it was true of the dead. And it was true too, a much more haunting thought, of all the personalities she had managed to assume and discard in a short life. No mythology could explain such a vanishing. Of the dead, it was said that the soul had left the body, a neat picture, implying that both were somewhere, separate but recognisable. The former selves, Evelyn as an undergraduate, Evelyn as a child, Evelyn as Geoffrey's mistress, had no such substance, and most of them were forgotten like dreams. The less she saw of people, the more she thought like this.

They pursued their quiet life in the hotel until a few weeks before Christmas. When Mr Gormann did die, it was undramatic and peaceful. She was sorry not to have been with him. It was while she was out on the Palace Pier one morning in the fog. Her walks had been getting later: what had begun as exercise taken after breakfast had become strolls before lunch.

It took her quite by surprise. She had been preparing herself for the event for weeks. Almost every time she went out, she told herself that she might not see him again. But it had not been so today. He was cheerful. They were reading some memoirs which were wittily written and which provoked reminiscence of his own. He had been eating well, and was enjoying his Campari as much as in the old days. He was also sprucing himself up a little – the leg was out of plaster now – in readiness for a visit next Saturday from Dicky Evans and Dodo. He had even spoken of paying calls himself, and, perhaps, of pottering around the Pavilion.

It was odd that he did not reply when she tapped on his door. Normally, he would cry out, "Enter, enter!" or, "Here comes the nurse-maid," or, "Come to see how the bomb victim is getting along?" There was silence now.

She never waited for an answer before entering. Knocking had just been a politeness to warn him that she was there. He sat in the chair by the window.

She hardly recognised him at first. Most startling, perhaps, was that he had totally changed colour. His ruddy complexion, the variety of colouring in his face, had disappeared altogether. He was an even, very pale yellow, with tips of absolute white about his nose and ears. The mouth was sunken: this also contributed to the unrecognisable look of the face. The corners of his lips had been pulled down, and they looked much thinner than in life. It looked as though his jaws were fixed on biting something which tasted unpleasant. The hair on his head, and his beard, seemed to have the stiffness of icicles.

She advanced before the sitting form, awestruck. She had never seen a corpse before at close quarters. It was neither frightening nor disgusting: she had prepared herself for either possibility. It was majestical. It was not really Mr Gormann. More baffling, even than Mr Gormann, a weird and statuesque presence had come to take his place: pale, snowy and still. Instinctively, she knelt before it, and kissed his hand.

The doctor described what had happened as "a mild heart attack". Evelyn felt that the phrase would aptly cover what had happened to herself in April in Kensington Gardens. Grief had not had time to sink in, but she knew that its painful process lay ahead. For the present, there was nothing to consider but arrangements.

She was shocked to discover in herself, actually, a sense of buoyancy, almost of cheerfulness, since he died. But this feeling was not unsullied by an agitation caused by the thought of Mr Gormann not having had time to alter the will.

Pimlico's face, when she met him at the airport, was drawn and unhappy. He spoke almost in a whisper, and his eyes were red. It was unthinkable, in such circumstances, that they should discuss the money, even though she had thought about little else since she found the stately corpse looking out to sea. As far as she knew "details" had not been finalised. There would be great awkwardness whatever happened, and she could not guess whether it would draw her closer to Pimlico or separate them altogether. At the moment, they clung to each other, like children lost in a labyrinth, neither of them knowing which way to turn, only saved from despair by one another's company.

The solicitor, Patterson, took over the arrangements for the funeral — it was a great relief to them both. Requiem Mass was to be celebrated in the Oratory three days after Mr Gormann's death.

In spite of his professed fondness for "discussing theology", Evelyn had never been able to discern whether the old man was religious. The subject never came up. He had certainly not been pious, but he had apparently stipulated that Catholic obsequies would be in order when he died.

It was odd to be returning to the church where she had been to a service with Jeremy that afternoon in the summer. Benediction he had called it. A letter came from him on the morning after Pimlico's arrival from Scotland — everything seemed to be happening at once. It was poignant that he concluded by sending his "love to Theo". News of the death would not reach him for weeks, and Evelyn did not know how it would affect him. It was a chatty letter, written from Trabzon, describing ruins, sunshine, mountain storms and monasteries. Allusions to his companion were frequent. "Angela and I bathed naked which was lovely," was what she thought it said. Reading it again, she thought it might have been "Angelo". It was impossible to read; and, really, she felt beyond caring about the gender of her brother's love mates.

When she had accompanied him to the Oratory, it had been almost empty, in spite of the fact that they were having that service. She wondered whether Mr Gormann and he had talked about the building when they had "discussed theology" at one of Pimlico's parties. Whatever doctrinal reasons the old man had for choosing this building for his funeral, it had an architectural appropriateness: large, absurdly foreign, theatrical, it was yet impossible to think of Knightsbridge without it. When she first came to live in its shadow, Geoffrey had told her that it was the Religious Department of Harrods, and having little sense of these things, she had believed him. She did not know what the religious department of a shop would sell, but it seemed likely that Harrods would have one. The feeling that the place had an obvious, if eccentric role, difficult to establish on first inspection, matched her feelings about Mr Gormann. It was possible that he had been one of the richest men in London. She did not know what to believe any more. But his role was conspicuously difficult to pin down. "What do you *do*?" – that dreadful question people ask at parties – could be answered in a hundred different ways on Mr Gormann's behalf without betraying a hint of what his life had been, still less, *who* he had been. Like a character in his beloved Browning, she thought of him as a grandiose "failure" who made one wonder what value one placed upon "success".

Dark, purply, Baroque, the great church reverberated around her as she sat next to Pimlico in a new black coat. There seemed to be a perpetual murmur echoing in the corners of the building. She found the place less alien than she had done before. The very familiarity of the waxy smell and flickering lights recalled the happiness of her afternoon with Jeremy, and brought a comfort of sorts.

Swathed in a velvet pall, surrounded by candles, as if it were in a State funeral, the coffin rested near the altar steps. The difficulty of forcing her mind to accept that this object contained Mr Gormann only emphasised the eery sense of his absence. Mr Gormann, at last, was nowhere. The huge church gave Evelyn no sense of his immortality; its high vacant dome, so full of nothingness, only intensified her awareness of death's mysterious finality. It was like a horrific game of Peep-bo: *now you see me, now you don't*. The face was never to emerge again.

There were far more people there than, had she devoted thought to the matter, she would have expected. The variety and multiplicity of the congregation was extraordinary. She kept looking over her shoulder to see people arrive: women, perhaps Saviours of Georgian Clapham, or Campaigners for Nuclear Disarmament, were there in almost as large numbers as men. The men ranged in age from people who looked as young as Jeremy to Mr Gormann's coevals. One or two uniforms were visible in the crowd. The occasional famous face could be discerned — front-bench politicians, actors, writers. The Swiss Ambassador was there, and the Warden of All Souls College, Oxford. Lady Antonia Fraser sat next to Mr Harris Thorning.

The impressiveness of Mr Gormann's circle had never really been made known to her before. She felt abashed at her insensitivity; the memory of her surprise that her father had heard of Mr Gormann came back to her. She wondered whether all these people had been kept in the dark about each other, as she had been of them; or whether his secretiveness was reserved for her.

"Theo's parties in the old days," occasionally alluded to by Pimlico Price in tones of mock-nostalgia, had presumably been attended by some of this crowd. "Theo is a believer in sausages on sticks," he said. "They were the only palatable feature of those evenings."

She thought of this article of faith during the singing of the Creed, no less opaque to her. She had expected the service itself to be moving. And there was, in its way, something undeniably impressive about a collection of people booming their expectation that an absent personage would not be delivered into the hands of the Evil One. But her inability to believe that Mr Gormann any longer existed produced a nervous blankness which stemmed even the desire to weep. Her chief anxiety was for Pimlico. An instinct to protect him crept over her, while the clergymen intoned and the choir sang.

"I shall be able to manage, after all," she thought, with no immediate reference to the money. The weeks in Brighton had prepared her for the event, although it was a shock when it came. Pimlico had no such assistance. For the first time in twenty years, he returned to London with no prospect of seeing Mr Gormann.

"Not a bad turn-out," was the first thing he said to her in the car on the way to the crematorium.

"Enormous."

"All Theo's lefty friends, of course."

"Were there?"

"And the conservationists. What an old clown he was."

They were silent for a while. She was not deceived by the jauntiness of his tone.

"The singing was very nice."

"Dicky Evans wasn't there, I notice," he continued. "Which more or less confirms one's suspicions of that front."

"Dodo said he had flu."

"Flu my arse. My bet is that Dicky has found out from someone that Patterson isn't the bloody fool Theo took him for. I spoke to him this morning on the telephone. The will is just as it was a year ago. Theo never actually signed anything, you know."

"But he must have done."

"Who said he must?"

The revision of her view of Pimlico's position had to be absolute after this disclosure. It silenced her. There was money in her bank account. She knew that. But the bulk of it . . . The implications of it were too much to take in all at once. Mental arithmetic, as the car glided towards Golders Green, told her nothing. It was not the sums involved which changed things, so much as her awareness that, far from needing to protect Pimlico, she was now in his power. The suspicion dawned on her that Mr Gormann had meant things to turn out this way. Her thoughts turned back to the evening in Fish Square when the old man had leant over the railings, a glass in hand, to watch Pimlico swimming with her in the pool.

She remembered once dining with Geoffrey in a restaurant. He had brought along a friend of his to meet her, a charming man in his twenties. They were both seated at the table when she arrived. At the end of the meal, during which conversation flowed, and she had got along very well with Geoffrey's friend, they had risen and the man had reached for his crutches. He had no legs.

Her reconsideration of Mr Gormann's motives provided a shock of the same order. There was no reason why she should not have looked back on the meal she had had with pleasure. Actually, when she saw she had been dining with a cripple, her feelings about it were totally altered; nor, quite, could she tell why. Nor was there any reason why her friendship with Mr Gormann, or her memories of it, should be changed by what was probably an over-dramatised distortion, induced by distress.

Only a few cars followed the coffin to the crematorium: just enough people to squeeze into the panelled "chapel" there. Two or three other funerals were arriving at the same time, and something of a queue developed at the entrance.

"You heard that they are flying the ashes back to Germany?" Pimlico said, as they waited to go in. Viewed in the light of what she had just learnt, he now seemed horribly in control of things. His rather thick lips, which she had assumed to be taut with grief, could equally be seen as firmly set, aggressive, confident. "Theo particularly wanted it. Touching in a way."

"He was always homesick really." The desire seemed a natural one to her. "He always felt out of place, displaced perhaps."

"Theo? I never noticed it."

"Didn't he ever talk to you about Heidelberg?"

"His University days, you mean. I wouldn't want to be sent back to Germany if I had been him." He paused. "Looks as if we're moving."

They began to trickle in. She felt more strongly than ever the impenetrable egotism of Pimlico. It almost offended her to hear him offer any judgment about Mr Gormann's emotions. Having built up a picture, satisfactory to herself, of the old man's nostalgia for his country, now apparently confirmed by the proposed destination of his ashes, it seemed ludicrous for Pimlico to venture an opinion of what he, in the circumstances, would have wanted. This fundamental lack of sympathy between the two men explained the "glass wall" which Mr Gormann used to speak of having grown up between them.

The coffin, now, without its pall, a tawdry sight, of pale polished oak, rested on a metal stand at the end of the chapel, spotlighted by pale blue lights of the sort which decorate cinemas. A vase of artificial flowers stood on the prayer desk next to it; the strains of "Abide with me" came from loudspeakers behind their heads.

The priest took his place at the prayer desk, and said a few prayers. Then he pressed a button, and the box glided away from them through a pair of tiny curtains. They shuffled together again when it was gone, recalling, for a moment, a miniature proscenium in a toy theatre. One half expected a large hand to appear, the size of the room itself, to dismantle the scenery, and return the puppets to their cupboard until they were required again.

Sleet, very faint, was falling as they emerged into the Garden of Remembrance. It was bitterly cold. What "remembrance" the scene provoked in her had nothing to do with Mr Gormann. It was all beginning to seem fantastic to her that he had entered her life at all. The last months had been dominated by him so absolutely that, now he was gone, she felt an instinct to go back to where she left off, to reconstruct the bits of life that were piecing themselves together before he came on the scene. She thought of her parents, and could almost weep for her desire to go back to them.

"Well, well," Pimlico was saying. "Quite a good send-off. But, God, I'm depressed. Let's go and get drunk."

"All right."

"And talk about 'us', eh? We haven't had a chance to plan things properly. Mother disapproves of long engagements. You do still want to go ahead, don't you, Evelyn?"

"I . . . yes. Yes, of course."

"Hullo, there's old Patterson over there. Better just have a word with him."

He left her standing by a rose-bed as he went off to talk to the lawyer. Evelyn would not have expected to be introduced to him, but one felt awkward, just standing in the cold. A chimney overhead gave out little billows of smoke.

She overheard snatches of their talk.

"A really wintry day . . . They did it all beautifully . . . A nice send-off . . ."

The lawyer climbed into a motor-car and drove away. Pimlico turned and strolled back to Evelyn. He looked satisfied, almost bumptious.

"I'm going to see Patterson tomorrow," he said. "He sent his regards to you."

"I could have come up and spoken to him, too, I suppose."

"Yes, I suppose you could."

"What else did he say?"

"Oh, just the usual things. And I told him about us. He sent his congratulations."

"Oh."

"Nice of him."

"Yes."

He took her hand and squeezed it gently as they stood, watching the lawyer's car disappearing through the sleet down the long avenue of cypress trees.

He fumbled in his pocket and held out a little roll of "Chewies".

"Have one," he said.

FOR THE BEST IN PAPERBACKS, LOOK FOR THE 🐧

In every corner of the world, on every subject under the sun, Penguin represents quality and variety – the very best in publishing today.

For complete information about books available from Penguin – including Pelicans, Puffins, Peregrines and Penguin Classics – and how to order them, write to us at the appropriate address below. Please note that for copyright reasons the selection of books varies from country to country.

In the United Kingdom: For a complete list of books available from Penguin in the U.K., please write to *Dept E.P., Penguin Books Ltd, Harmondsworth, Middlesex, UB7 0DA*

In the United States: For a complete list of books available from Penguin in the U.S., please write to *Dept BA, Penguin, 299 Murray Hill Parkway, East Rutherford, New Jersey 07073*

In Canada: For a complete list of books available from Penguin in Canada, please write to *Penguin Books Canada Ltd, 2801 John Street, Markham, Ontario L3R 1B4*

In Australia: For a complete list of books available from Penguin in Australia, please write to the *Marketing Department, Penguin Books Australia Ltd, P.O. Box 257, Ringwood, Victoria 3134*

In New Zealand: For a complete list of books available from Penguin in New Zealand, please write to the *Marketing Department, Penguin Books (NZ) Ltd, Private Bag, Takapuna, Auckland 9*

In India: For a complete list of books available from Penguin, please write to *Penguin Overseas Ltd, 706 Eros Apartments, 56 Nehru Place, New Delhi, 110019*

In Holland: For a complete list of books available from Penguin in Holland, please write to *Penguin Books Nederland B.V., Postbus 195, NL–1380AD Weesp, Netherlands*

In Germany: For a complete list of books available from Penguin, please write to *Penguin Books Ltd, Friedrichstrasse 10 – 12, D–6000 Frankfurt Main 1, Federal Republic of Germany*

In Spain: For a complete list of books available from Penguin in Spain, please write to *Longman Penguin España, Calle San Nicolas 15, E–28013 Madrid, Spain*

Also by A. N. Wilson in Penguins

THE HEALING ART

Winner of the Somerset Maugham Award, the Southern Arts Literature Prize and the Arts Council National Book Award.

Pamela Cowper is facing death. Not a vague probability, but a shockingly imminent oblivion from cancer. How will she face it?

Dorothy Higgs, on the other hand, is told that she will live to be one of her doctor's success stories. And, as the two women confront their destinies across the gulfs of fear and hope, fate, as always, reserves the final twist until the end.

'Not a page goes by without our being astounded' – John Braine in the *Sunday Telegraph*

'I could never have enough of it' – Auberon Waugh in the *Evening Standard*

WHO WAS OSWALD FISH?

Well, who *was* Oswald Fish? Find out in this novel that froths and hums with Rabelaisian farce and rumbustious sex . . . a book that William Boyd has described as 'the comic novel at its most mature and impressive; an amused and entertaining – but at the core, serious – commentary on the vanities and pretensions of the human condition.'

'A. N. Wilson is a master at playing black comedy that can make us laugh just when we should cry' – *New Statesman*

and

Wise Virgin
Scandal
How Can We Know?
Gentlemen in England
Hilaire Belloc

A CHOICE OF PENGUIN FICTION

Maia Richard Adams

The heroic romance of love and war in an ancient empire from one of our greatest storytellers. 'Enormous and powerful' – *Financial Times*

The Warning Bell Lynne Reid Banks

A wonderfully involving, truthful novel about the choices a woman must make in her life – and the price she must pay for ignoring the counsel of her own heart. 'Lynne Reid Banks knows how to get to her reader: this novel grips like Super Glue' – *Observer*

Doctor Slaughter Paul Theroux

Provocative and menacing – a brilliant dissection of lust, ambition and betrayal in 'civilized' London. 'Witty, chilly, exuberant, graphic' – *The Times Literary Supplement*. Now filmed as *Half Moon Street*.

Wise Virgin A. N. Wilson

Giles Fox's work on the Pottle manuscript, a little-known thirteenth-century tract on virginity, leads him to some innovative research on the subject that takes even his breath away. 'A most elegant and chilling comedy' – *Observer* Books of the Year

Last Resorts Clare Boylan

Harriet loved Joe Fisher for his ordinariness – for his ordinary suits and hats, his ordinary money and his ordinary mind, even for his ordinary wife. 'An unmitigated delight' – *Time Out*

Trade Wind M. M. Kaye

An enthralling blend of history, adventure and romance from the author of the bestselling *The Far Pavilions*

A CHOICE OF PENGUIN FICTION

Other Women Lisa Alther

From the bestselling author of *Kinflicks* comes this compelling novel of today's woman – and a heroine with whom millions of women will identify.

Your Lover Just Called John Updike

Stories of Joan and Richard Maple – a couple multiplied by love and divided by lovers. Here is the portrait of a modern American marriage in all its mundane moments and highs and lows of love as only John Updike could draw it.

Mr Love and Justice Colin MacInnes

Frankie Love took up his career as a ponce about the same time as Edward Justice became vice-squad detective. Except that neither man was particularly suited for his job, all they had in common was an interest in crime. But, as any ponce or copper will tell you, appearances are not always what they seem. Provocative and honest and acidly funny, *Mr Love and Justice* is the final volume of Colin MacInnes's famous London trilogy.

An Ice-Cream War William Boyd

As millions are slaughtered on the Western Front, a ridiculous and little-reported campaign is being waged in East Africa – a war they continued after the Armistice because no one told them to stop. 'A towering achievement' – John Carey, Chairman of the Judges of the 1982 Booker Prize, for which this novel was shortlisted.

Every Day is Mother's Day Hilary Mantel

An outrageous story of lust, adultery, madness, death and the social services. 'Strange . . . rather mad . . . extremely funny . . . she sometimes reminded me of the early Muriel Spark' – Auberon Waugh

1982 Janine Alasdair Gray

Set inside the head of an ageing, divorced, alcoholic, insomniac supervisor of security installations who is tippling in the bedroom of a small Scottish hotel – this is a most brilliant and controversial novel.

A CHOICE OF PENGUIN FICTION

A Fanatic Heart   Edna O'Brien

'A selection of twenty-nine stories (including four new ones) full of wit and feeling and savagery that prove that Edna O'Brien is one of the subtlest and most lavishly gifted writers we have' – A. Alvarez in the *Observer*

Charade   John Mortimer

'Wonderful comedy . . . an almost Firbankian melancholy . . . John Mortimer's hero is helplessly English' – *Punch*. 'What is *Charade*? Comedy? Tragedy? Mystery? It is all three and more' – *Daily Express*

Casualties   Lynne Reid Banks

'The plot grips; the prose is fast-moving and elegant; above all, the characters are wincingly, winningly human . . . if literary prizes were awarded for craftsmanship and emotional directness, *Casualties* would head the field' – *Daily Telegraph*

The Anatomy Lesson   Philip Roth

The hilarious story of Nathan Zuckerman, the famous forty-year-old writer who decides to give it all up and become a doctor – and a pornographer – instead. 'The finest, boldest and funniest piece of fiction which Philip Roth has yet produced' – *Spectator*

Gabriel's Lament   Paul Bailey

Shortlisted for the 1986 Booker Prize
'The best novel yet by one of the most careful fiction craftsmen of his generation' – *Guardian*. 'A magnificent novel, moving, eccentric and unforgettable. He has a rare feeling for language and an understanding of character which few can rival' – *Daily Telegraph*

Small Changes   Marge Piercy

In the Sixties the world seemed to be making big changes – but for many women it was the small changes that were the hardest and the most profound. *Small Changes* is Marge Piercy's explosive new novel about women fighting to make their way in a man's world.